THE
PAPER
DRAGON

THE PAPER DRAGON

• A RAGGEDY ANN • ADVENTURE

Written and Illustrated by JOHNNY GRUELLE

SIMON & SCHUSTER BOOKS FOR YOUNG READERS

New York   London   Toronto   Sydney   Singapore

PUBLISHER'S NOTE:

Simon & Schuster Books for Young Readers is proud to be reissuing this American classic in the format in which it was originally published. The color illustrations have been reproduced from those in the early printings, thus restoring the delicacy and detail that were lost as the plates deteriorated over many printings. We have restored the endpapers and the jacket to their original condition and, as in that edition, there are no page numbers or table of contents. The book is printed on acid-free paper for permanence and signature-sewn in the traditional manner for ease of use.

 SIMON & SCHUSTER BOOKS FOR YOUNG READERS
An imprint of Simon & Schuster Children's Publishing Division
1230 Avenue of the Americas, New York, New York 10020
Copyright 1926 by The P. F. Volland Company
Copyright renewed 1954 by Simon & Schuster, Inc.
First Simon & Schuster Books for Young Readers Edition 2003

The text for this book is set in Caslon Old Face.
Manufactured in China
10 9 8 7 6 5 4 3 2 1
Library of Congress Cataloging-in-Publication Data
Gruelle, Johnny, 1880-1938.
The paper dragon : a Raggedy Ann adventure / written and illustrated by Johnny Gruelle.
p. cm.
Originally published: New York : P.F. Volland, 1926.
Summary: When Raggedy Ann and Raggedy Andy set out to help a little girl find her father, they meet up with a mean couple, a paper dragon, and a two-headed dog before ending up at a magic castle.
ISBN 0-689-84969-9 (alk. paper)
[1. Dolls—Fiction. 2. Wishes—Fiction. 3. Magic—Fiction.] Title.
PZ7.G9324 Pap 2003
[Fic]—dc21   2002067034

To
EVELYN, DAVID,
and
JUDY CHAMBERS

*With the wish that their pathway
through life may be bordered with
the flowers of friendship.*

JOHNNY GRUELLE
Norwalk, Connecticut
September 2, 1925

CHAPTER ONE

RAGGEDY Ann and Raggedy Andy were two rag dolls. They were stuffed with nice clean white cotton and their faces were painted on them. Both Raggedy Ann and Raggedy Andy wore very cheery smiles and were friendly, happy little creatures.

The two Raggedys lived in the nursery at Marcella's house and always had great fun with the other dolls, for as you surely must know, dolls play together when there are no real for sure people around to watch them. And although Raggedy Ann and Raggedy Andy loved all the other dolls in the nursery very much, still at times they liked to leave the nursery and walk down through the deep, deep woods filled with fairies 'n everything, because there they found strange adventures.

Once before, in adventuring in the deep, deep woods Raggedy Ann and Raggedy Andy had found a very magical stick. It was a wishing stick and made every wish come true. This stick had been sewed inside Raggedy Andy's cotton stuffed body and just looking at him, no one would guess he could make wishes come true.

Raggedy Ann had been as fortunate as Raggedy Andy, for on one adventure in the deep, deep woods, Raggedy Ann had found a very Magical Wishing Pebble, and this was sewed up inside her cotton stuffed body, so that Raggedy

Ann, like Raggedy Andy, could make her wishes come true too. So, this day, when the two Raggedys kissed the other dolls in the nursery good-bye and skipped out through the garden gate and down the path leading to the deep, deep woods, their little cotton stuffed bodies tingled with excitement, for they both felt they were running to meet some wonderful adventures. And indeed, this was true. The Raggedys had gone but a short distance into the deep, deep woods when Raggedy Andy heard something.

"Didn't that sound like some one calling for help?" Raggedy Andy asked as he caught Raggedy Ann's arm.

"I heard something, but I could not hear just what was said," Raggedy Ann replied in a whisper.

"Listen," Raggedy Andy said. "There it is again!"

"HELP! HELP!" some one cried.

"It's over the other side of that great big stone," Raggedy Ann whispered. "Let's run over real easy and climb on the stone, then we can see who it is."

The two Raggedys caught hold of hands and ran over to the large stone and when they reached it they saw little steps leading to the top. Up the steps they climbed until they could look over the top of the great stone.

"I've got you this time," a voice said. "And this time I will not let you get away."

"Oh, please Mister Doodle, don't take me to your house and make me chop the wood for you! I have to run to the store to get a penny's worth of needle eyes for mama and hurry right back so she can finish her sewing. Then I have to—"

"HA! You won't run to the store today," Mister Doodle laughed. "I've got a lot of wood to be chopped and I am too tired to do it myself so you got to do it!"

"You are a mean man, Mister Doodle, and I just bet you had better run along home and chop the wood yourself before you get in trouble," Raggedy Ann said from the top of the stone.

"Is that so?" Mister Doodle laughed "I guess I will take Marggy home to chop my wood if I want to." And Mister Doodle started to pull the little girl along behind him through the woods.

"Now I'll tell you what, Mister Doodle," cried Raggedy Ann. "If you do not let go of Marggy before I count three, you'll find yourself standing on your head."

"Ha! Ha! Ha!" Mister Doodle laughed, for you see, he did not know that all Raggedy Ann or Andy had to do was to make a wish and the wish would come true, "I'd like to see a rag doll keep me from taking Marggy home to chop the wood for me!"

"ONE," said Raggedy Ann, "two", she added after a pause, "now you better let go," she warned. But Mister Doodle gave Marggy a pull and started away.

"Alright," said Raggedy Ann. "THREE!"

"And I wish that he bumps up and down real hard," said Raggedy Andy as Mister Doodle turned upside down and stood upon his head.

"Oh! You must be fairies!" Marggy cried as she saw Mister Doodle do just as the two Raggedys had wished.

"No, we are only two rag dolls, Marggy," Raggedy Ann said as she and Andy jumped from the large stone. "Now let's run to your house before Mister Doodle gets upon his feet again!" And catching Marggy's hands, the two Raggedys ran through the woods until they came to a little house with an open door.

"Ha!" said someone over by the fireplace.

"Is that your mother, Marggy?" Raggedy Ann asked as she saw a woman in an easy chair watching a pot hanging over cold ashes.

"Dear me, no!" Marggy replied. "I tried to tell you this was Mister Doodle's house, but you ran so fast I could not catch my breath."

"Then is that Missus Doodle?" Raggedy Andy asked.

"Yes, I am," Missus Doodle said. "And you are just in time too. I want to get supper and the food won't cook, because I have no fire. One of you carry some wood in from the other room and light it. Mister Doodle will be here in a minute."

Marggy started to get the wood for Missus Doodle, but Raggedy Andy stopped her. "How long have you been sitting here watching that pot, Mrs. Doodle?"

"Ever since early this morning," Mrs. Doodle replied. "But what has that to do with getting the wood?"

"It hasn't anything to do with it," Raggedy Andy replied. "Except that we will not get the wood for you when you try to make us do it. If you had asked one of us real nice, we would have been pleased to get the wood and start the fire."

"Then into the cage you go!" cried Mrs. Doodle as she jumped out of her chair and caught Raggedy Andy.

"Here!" Marggy cried as she caught Mrs. Doodle's arm. "You put Raggedy Andy down right away!"

Mrs. Doodle walked out into the other room and stuffed

Raggedy Andy into an empty parrot cage hanging on the wall. Then she ran after Raggedy Ann and when she caught her, she stuffed Raggedy Ann in beside Raggedy Andy.

"Polly wants a cracker!" Raggedy Andy cried just like a parrot.

"Now!" Mrs. Doodle cried as she gave Marggy's ear a twist, "get busy and build the fire!" And she pushed the little girl into the wood room.

"Bang! Bang! Bang!" someone knocked on the front door.

"Who is it?" asked Mrs. Doodle as she walked to the door.

"It's me, Mr. Doodle! Just wait until I catch Raggedy Ann and Raggedy Andy and Marggy!"

"Ha! Ha! Ha!" Mrs. Doodle laughed. "Then come right in for the two Raggedys are in the parrot cage!"

"Ha," Mr. Doodle said as he picked up a stick. "Show me where they are."

"Polly wants a cracker!" Raggedy Andy cried from the parrot cage just like a parrot.

"Maybe you should not tease him, Raggedy Andy," Raggedy Ann said.

Raggedy Andy just laughed when Mr. Doodle walked in the room. "You just watch, Raggedy Ann," he whispered. Then he cried to Mr. Doodle, "Hello Mr. Doodle, how did it feel to dance around on your head?"

Mr. Doodle was very, very angry. "I'll show you now that you are fastened up in the parrot cage! I'll hit the cage with this big stick and knock it off the nail, then the cage will fall on the floor and you will both bump your heads!"

Mr. Doodle threw the big stick right at the cage, but Raggedy Andy, who had a wishing stick sewed inside his rag body made a wish the moment Mr. Doodle came in the house. So when Mr. Doodle threw the stick, instead of the stick knocking the parrot cage from the nail, the stick circled around the parrot cage and came flying back at Mr. Doodle's head.

"Wow!" Mr. Doodle cried as the stick knocked his hat off his head. "What made that stick bounce that way?"

"You didn't hit the parrot cage, that's why," said Mrs. Doodle.

Mr. Doodle picked up the stick and took careful aim. "This time I'll knock the cage down and bump the Raggedys' heads, I'll bet a nickel!"

And he threw the stick so hard that when it circled around the parrot cage again, it sailed right back and cracked Mr. Doodle on top of his head. This made Mr. Doodle sit down on the floor so hard he jarred a vase off the mantel piece.

"Now see what you did!" Mrs. Doodle cried as she hit Mr. Doodle with the broom. "You broke my nicest vase! I'll hit the cage this time and bump the Raggedys' heads." Then Mrs. Doodle threw the broom at the parrot cage, but the broom circled around the edge just as the stick had done and after striking Mrs. Doodle and knocking her down, it flew along the wall and knocked down three pictures.

Raggedy Ann and Raggedy Andy in the parrot cage had to hold their rag sides to keep from laughing, for the harder Mr. and Mrs. Doodle tried to knock down the parrot cage, the more damage they did until finally their whole house was covered with broken vases and pictures and broken dishes and both of them had a lot of bumps on the top of their heads.

"You see," Raggedy Andy said from the parrot cage. "Whenever you try to injure another, you always harm yourselves. Let this be a lesson to you!"

Now this made Raggedy Ann and Raggedy Andy feel sorry, for although the Doodles had tried to injure the Raggedys, still the Raggedys did not wish to injure the Doodles in return. So Raggedy Andy made a wish that all the broken things would be mended right away. And soon everything was just as good as new.

Then when Mr. and Mrs. Doodle saw everything was not broken, they could not understand what had happened, for you see, they did not know that every time the Raggedys made a wish, the wish came true.

"I guess we must have been dreaming," Mr. Doodle said as he got up from the floor.

"I guess we were," Mrs. Doodle said.

"No, you were not dreaming," Raggedy Andy said. "You will find that every time you try to injure another, you will hurt yourself twice as much."

Now Mr. and Mrs. Doodle did not believe this was true, so they said, "The Raggedys must have a magic charm in their pockets, for every time they make a wish, the wish comes true. So we must take the magic charms away from them, and then we can make all our wishes come true."

"The first thing I shall wish for will be a big piano, then I will sit and play pretty music all day long," said Mrs. Doodle.

"Indeed!" Mr. Doodle replied. "I shall have the first wish. I shall wish for an automobile!"

Then the Doodles stamped their feet and pulled each other's noses. While they were quarreling, Raggedy Ann and Raggedy Andy jumped out of the parrot cage, opened the door real easy and slipped outside.

"Oh dear," Raggedy Ann said as she stopped running, "We ran away from the Doodles' house and left Marggy there! Now the Doodles will be so angry when they find we have escaped, they will make Marggy chop all their wood and build their fires and do their cooking!"

"Then we must hurry right back and take Marggy away from Mr. Doodle's house," said Raggedy Andy as he turned back.

When the Raggedys came to Mr. and Mrs. Doodle's house they could hear a lot of noise inside so they walked right in without knocking.

"You must let me run home to my Mama," Marggy said to Mr. Doodle.

"Not until you chop up all the wood for us and make the fire and do the cooking," Mr. Doodle said. "Mrs. Doodle and I are too tired to do it." Then Mr. Doodle caught hold of the little girl's arm and pulled her to the wood pile. "There now," he said as he shut the door. "Don't come out until the wood is all chopped."

Marggy sat down in a corner of the wood room and began crying, for she was too small to chop wood. But Raggedy Ann and Raggedy Andy had slipped into the room when Mr. Doodle wasn't looking, so they wiped Marggy's tears away and said, "Don't cry, Marggy, we will rescue you some way."

"But Mr. Doodle has locked the door tight," said Marggy. "And we can't get out!"

Raggedy Ann peeped through the key hole and saw Mr. and Mrs. Doodle sitting in easy chairs. "We will rest while Marggy chops the wood," said Mrs. Doodle.

"Ha! Ha!" Raggedy Ann thought to herself. 'If you are that lazy, it will just serve you right if we can fool you." And she thought and thought until she ripped two stitches in the top of her rag head, then she made a wish. It was a queer wish. Raggedy Ann wished that she and Raggedy Andy and Marggy were only as large as tiny little weeny weeny bugs. And just as soon as the wish came true, the three of them walked right out through the crack under the back door. Next Raggedy Ann made a wish that they would become large again. Then they caught hold of hands and ran for Marggy's house as fast as they could go.

"The joke I played on Mr. and Mrs. Doodle was a good one," Raggedy Ann laughed. "After we escaped from the Doodles' house, I wished that all the wood would grow larger! Now when Mr. Doodle finds he has to chop it after

all, he will have more work to do!"

"And that will serve him just right too," Raggedy Andy laughed. "For whenever anyone puts off doing a thing, hoping that someone else will come along and do it for him, he always finds that the work seems harder."

"You should tell your Daddy to speak to Mr. Doodle," said Raggedy Ann to Marggy.

"Oh, dear me," Marggy replied. "I haven't any Daddy. He went out in the woods a long time ago and never came back."

"Well, well, well," the Raggedys both said. "Then we must search for him and maybe we can find him and bring him home to you and your Mama."

CHAPTER TWO

WHEN Marggy told her Mama that the Raggedys were going to search for her Daddy she was very happy.

"I tell you what let's do," said Raggedy Ann. "Let's take a ball of your Mama's darning cotton and make a wish that the cotton will roll in front of us until it comes to where your Daddy is."

Even Marggy's Mama thought this would be lots of fun, so she got a ball of red cotton and Raggedy Ann made the wish. "Now we will follow the pretty red ball until it rolls to your Daddy," said Raggedy Ann.

"I believe we had better take some cream puffs and doughnuts with us," Marggy's Mama said. "For we may get hungry." So she filled a basket with doughnuts and cream puffs, then they all followed the red ball as it rolled through the woods.

After the red ball had rolled along for almost a mile our friends came to a little house beside the path and just as the red ball came to the front door, a funny little old woman ran out and caught it.

"Oh my!" Raggedy Ann said. "You mustn't pick up the little red ball! We are following it!"

Then the funny little old woman made a face at Raggedy

Ann. "I found it!" she cried. "I need some red cotton to mend my red stockings!"

"Oh dear! What shall we do?" Marggy's Mama asked.

"There isn't anything you can do!" the funny little old woman replied. "The red cotton is mine now!" And with this, she started into the house with the little red ball.

Now maybe you don't know it, but when Raggedy Ann made the wish for the red ball to roll in front of them, this made the little red ball a magical ball, so when the funny little old woman tried to take the ball into her house, the magic ball pulled just as hard in the opposite direction.

My! How the funny little old woman tussled. She pulled and the ball pulled until finally the ball pulled the hardest and it pulled the funny little old woman right down the path in front of our friends.

"If you do not let go of the little red ball, you will wear all the soles off your shoes," Raggedy Ann said.

"I will never, never let go!" cried the funny little old woman.

The funny little old woman was very determined and she held on to the little red ball, even when it pulled her along and made her feet slide over the gravel. "You will wear out your nice shoes," Marggy's Mama said.

"I don't care!" cried the funny little old woman. "You will have to buy me new ones!"

"Did you ever hear the like!" Raggedy Andy exclaimed. "Here the funny little old woman tries to take our magical ball and when she can't take it, she blames us if she wears out her shoes scuffing along!"

The funny little old woman held her feet out in front of her and just slid along the path, and this held the little red ball back just enough so that Raggedy Ann and Raggedy Andy and Marggy and her Mama had to walk real slow or else step upon the funny little old woman's heels.

"I guess we'll have to help the little red ball," Raggedy Andy said. "It has a hard time pulling the funny little old woman along. I'll help the ball by pushing the funny little old woman."

But when Raggedy Andy helped the little red ball by pushing on the funny little old woman, she slid over the gravel in the path so fast, it made her feet burn, so she sat right down plunk in the path and wouldn't budge a speck.

"Now what shall we do?" Raggedy Andy asked as he scratched his head.

"I shan't budge!" the funny little old woman cried. "This little red ball is mine and I shall take it home!"

"I feel like boxing her ears," Marggy's Mama cried. "The funny little old woman is just like a spoilt child, and it would teach her a lesson if some one paddywhacked her."

"Maybe after she rests awhile she will stand up again," said Raggedy Andy. "Then the little red ball will pull her along."

So while they waited for the funny little old woman to stand up, Marggy's Mama got out the cream puffs and doughnuts.

"We'll give you a doughnut, if you'd like one," Raggedy Ann said to the funny little old woman. But the funny little old woman just shook her head and held tightly to the little red ball.

"I shall hang on to the little red magic ball until I can take it home with me," the funny little old woman said. "I need some red yarn to darn my stockings with."

"But if you do not let go of the little red magic ball, you will wear the soles off your shoes scuffing along," said Raggedy Andy. "Then you'll have to go to the shoe maker and have new soles put on your shoes."

"Maybe when we come to a brook, the little red ball will pull the funny little old woman right into the water," Marggy said.

But even when they came to a little brook, the funny little old woman held to the little red magic ball. It pulled her right through the water so she was wet up to her knees.

"Dear me," Raggedy Ann said. "We will never find Marggy's Daddy if the funny little old woman keeps holding the magic ball back all the time! We would have been miles farther if the ball had been allowed to roll along as fast as it started."

"Maybe if I carried the funny little old woman she wouldn't pull back on the magic ball all the time," said Raggedy Andy.

So Raggedy Andy picked up the funny little old woman and started to carry her the way the little red magic ball wanted to go, but she kicked and twisted and wiggled and scolded so hard, she knocked Raggedy Andy right over backwards. And when Raggedy Andy fell down, the funny little old woman bumped her head on a stone so hard, she forgot all about holding the little red magic ball and held her head instead.

"It was all your fault!" she cried to Raggedy Andy. "If you had not tried to carry me, I would not have bumped my head!"

"I'm sorry," Raggedy Andy said, for he would not have had the funny little old woman bump her head on purpose. "But now you have let go of our little red magic ball and we can follow it and find Marggy's Daddy, I will give you a nice big ball of red cotton."

The funny little old woman was so pleased she dried her tears and ran right home.

CHAPTER THREE

RAGGEDY ANN and Raggedy Andy and Marggy and her Mama followed the little red magical ball of darning cotton through the woods until they came to a gate made of logs. The little red magical ball rolled through the gate and our friends started to follow it, when a great big Dragon, just like the Dragons you see in Chinese pictures, came right out and opened its mouth and the little red magical ball of darning cotton rolled inside.

"Oh, dear!" cried Marggy's Mama as she sat down on a stone and wiped her eyes with her apron. "Now the little red magical ball is gone and we will never find Daddy."

"Why did you swallow our little red magical ball of darning cotton?" Raggedy Ann asked the great big dragon.

"Because," the Dragon replied.

"That isn't any reason at all," Raggedy Ann said. "And you ought to be ashamed of yourself! That's what!"

"Well, I'm not," the great big large Dragon replied as it wiggled its long tail. And when Raggedy Ann pointed her rag hand at its nose to make it feel ashamed of itself, the great big large Dragon opened its great large mouth real wide and went, "Gobble! Gobble!"

"Here! You stop that, Mister Dragon!" Raggedy Andy cried, but he was too late for the great big large Dragon had swallowed Raggedy Ann completely.

"Now then, you've gone and done it!" Raggedy Andy cried as he hunted around for a great big stick.

"What are you going to do with that great big stick?" the Dragon asked as he twirled his long tail.

"You just wait and see! That's what!" Raggedy Andy said as he rolled up his sleeves.

"Are we going to have a fight?" the Dragon asked.

Raggedy Andy did not answer the Dragon. Instead, he walked right up to it holding the large stick in front of him. When Raggedy Andy came up to him, the Dragon opened his great big mouth and started to say "Gobble!" Gobble!" just like he had done when he swallowed Raggedy Ann, but Raggedy Andy was too smart for him. Raggedy Andy just as quick as a wink, put the large stick in the Dragon's mouth and this held the Dragon's mouth wide open.

My! How the Dragon wiggled and wobbled his long tail, but it did no good, for he could not get the stick out of his mouth. And when he wiggled and wobbled his long tail Raggedy Andy and Marggy and her Mama could hear Raggedy Ann and the little red magical ball rattling around way back inside the Dragon. Then they heard a funny scratching sound and here came Raggedy Ann crawling out.

"The Dragon is just made out of paper and thin slats of wood!" Raggedy Ann laughed.

"The reason I did not fight the great big large Dragon was because I saw right away that he was made out of paper," said Raggedy Andy. "And if I had hit him upon the head with the large stick, I would have broken his head in pieces."

"Are you going to take the stick out of his mouth?" Marggy's Mama asked Raggedy Andy, "The great big Dragon might eat someone else up just as he did Raggedy Ann."

Raggedy Ann laughed. "The great big Dragon wouldn't harm anyone even if he did swallow them," she said. "For he is hollow all the way to the tip of his tail. And if he swallowed anyone, all they would have to do would be to kick real hard and they could kick a large hole right through him."

Raggedy Andy walked up to the large paper Dragon and took the big stick out of its mouth. "There," said Raggedy Andy. "Does that feel better?"

"Yes indeed!" the Dragon replied. "When my mouth was propped open with the stick, it made cold chills run all the way to the tip end of my long tail, and it felt just like someone had left the front door wide open on a cold day."

"Then after this, you mustn't swallow anyone again," said Raggedy Andy.

"I did not swallow Raggedy Ann," the Dragon replied.

"No, he didn't, that's true," Raggedy Ann agreed. "I jumped into his mouth, because I saw right away he was made out of paper and thin slats of wood. I knew someone had to rescue the little red magical ball of darning cotton or we would never find Marggy's Daddy."

"What do you eat, Mister Dragon?" Marggy's Mama asked as she walked up and thumped the Dragon's head to see if he really and truly was paper.

"I never eat anything," the Dragon replied, "But lots of times when I yawn the wind blows pieces of paper right in my mouth and dry leaves and I do not know how to get them out again! I'm afraid maybe if mice find out I have pieces of paper and nice dry leaves in me, they might build nests in my paper body. And you know how mice are, sometimes they chew holes in things."

"I tell you what let's do! Let's pull him up into a tree by the tip end of his tail and shake all the leaves and pieces of paper out," Raggedy Andy said.

Marggy and her Mama couldn't climb trees like Raggedy Ann and Raggedy Andy, so they stayed upon the ground and boosted the paper Dragon's tail up to Raggedy Ann and Andy. Then Raggedy Ann and Raggedy Andy shook the paper Dragon's tail until all the leaves and pieces of paper rattled down to his mouth. Then Marggy and her Mama cleaned all the leaves and paper out of the paper Dragon's mouth and he felt very, very much better.

Then Raggedy Ann and Raggedy Andy and Marggy and her Mama told the paper Dragon good-bye and followed the little red magical ball of darning cotton through the woods.

CHAPTER FOUR

RAGGEDY ANN and Raggedy Andy and Marggy and her Mama had gone only a short way when they heard a loud noise in back of them.

"Land sakes!" cried Raggedy Ann. "What can be making all that racket?" But because the others did not know, of course they could not tell, so they just had to wait until whatever made the racket reached them.

The noise grew louder and louder until they saw the paper Dragon coming through the woods as fast as he could wiggle. The paper Dragon wiggled and twisted along so fast his long tail bumped against the trees blumpity smack, crash, blump!

"Dear me! Something must be wrong with the paper Dragon!" Raggedy Ann said. "He will tear a lot of holes in his sides if he isn't careful the way he smacks into the trees and stones!"

The paper Dragon was so out of breath when he reached Raggedy Ann all he could say was "Run!" And he said it with such a wheeze no one could understand what he said.

"Whatever made you wiggle so fast through the woods, Mister Dragon?" Raggedy Andy asked. "You've snagged a lot of holes in your tail, and while you rest we will mend them with paper and glue."

"But we haven't any glue!" Marggy's Mama said.

"Maybe we can use the cream out of a cream puff!" Raggedy Ann suggested. And as there were lots of pieces of paper blowing about through the woods Raggedy Ann and Raggedy Andy soon stuck patches on every hole in the paper Dragon's body.

"Ah! That feels ever so much better," the paper Dragon said. "I guess the reason I got out of breath was because I had so many holes in my long body, and the air leaked out of the holes."

"Maybe you ran with your mouth open," Marggy said.

"Yes, that's true," the Dragon replied. "Let's see now, what was I going to tell you? I guess it slipped out of the holes, for I have completely forgotten what it was."

"Try to think real hard," suggested Raggedy Andy. "Raggedy Ann and I often think so hard we rip stitches out of our heads."

"But I have no stitches in my head," the Dragon replied.

"Then we'll just sit here and wait until you think without ripping any stitches," said Raggedy Ann.

So the Raggedys and Marggy and her Mama sat down and waited for the Dragon to remember.

"Can't you remember what it was?" Raggedy Andy asked after they had sat there awhile.

"I haven't the least idea," the paper Dragon replied. "I can't seem to think very well."

"Maybe if you would scratch your head, it would help," said Raggedy Ann.

"Oh, he can't scratch his head," Raggedy Andy laughed. "He hasn't any hands to scratch with."

"Of course not," Raggedy Ann laughed. "It was silly of me to suggest it!"

"But we could take sticks and scratch his head for him," Marggy said.

"Maybe that will help," the paper Dragon said.

So Raggedy Ann and Raggedy Andy and Marggy and her Mama each got a stick and scratched the Dragon's head.

After they had scratched awhile, the paper Dragon said, "That's enough! I remember what it was now! You must run and run fast!"

"But why should we run?" Raggedy Ann asked. "If we run, we will get ahead of the little magical red ball of darning cotton and you know, the little red ball rolls through the woods and is leading us to where Marggy's Daddy is."

"Well, you had better run anyway!" the Dragon said. "For there's a queer man running after you, and the only reason he isn't here now is because I wiggled through the woods so much faster than he can run."

"Who is it?" Raggedy Ann asked of the others.

"I'll tell you who it is," the Dragon said. "It's Mr. Doodle!"

"Oh dear!" Marggy cried. "He wants to take me back to his house to chop wood for him!"

"Well, he will never do that," Raggedy Andy said. "We will hide some place and wait until he runs by, then we will go another way."

"Here's a dandy place to hide," said Raggedy Ann. "Quick! Everyone get in this great big hollow tree. Afterwards we will catch up with the magic ball."

So they all squeezed into the great big hollow tree. Even the Dragon, and waited for Mr. Doodle to run by them.

"Here he comes now, I can hear him!" the Dragon said to Raggedy Ann and Raggedy Andy and Marggy and her Mama. The Dragon was the last to crawl into the great big hollow tree so he could hear better than the others.

"He's coming lickety split through the woods," the Dragon whispered.

"Goody! Now he's going by! It's stuffy in here all crowded together and I will be glad when Mr. Doodle runs past," said Raggedy Ann.

"Oh shucks!" the Dragon cried out loud.

"Be quiet!" Raggedy Ann said. "He will hear you sure!"

"That's just it!" the Dragon said. "He has heard us and he is pulling and yanking my tail now!"

"He's pulling me out of the tree!" the Dragon wailed.

Indeed, this was true, for the others soon felt the Dragon slipping and slipping until suddenly he was yanked right out of the great big hollow tree.

"Ha! Ha! Ha!" laughed Mr. Doddle. "You thought you could fool me did you?"

"How did you know where we were?" Raggedy Andy asked as he and the others came out.

"Why, who wouldn't know where you were when the foolish Dragon had ten or fifteen feet of his tail sticking out of the tree!"

"I knew I would spoil it all, if I hid in the tree with you! I'm so sorry!" the Dragon cried.

"Don't you care," Raggedy Andy whispered. "You did the best you knew how and we are glad of that."

"Now," said Mr. Doddle. "I've come to take Marggy home with me to chop the wood."

"Dear me," Raggedy Ann exclaimed. "If you worked as hard chopping your wood as you have chasing us, you would have the wood all chopped!"

"I'm too tired to chop wood, I tell you," Mr. Doddle shouted as he gave Marggy's arm a pull.

"Now see here," the Dragon cried. "I guess we will have to fight!" So Mr. Doddle took off his coat and rolled up his sleeves. "The rest of you had better keep back out of the way," he said.

So Raggedy Ann passed the doughnuts and cream puffs. "For," she said as they took seats back out of the way. "We might as well have lunch while we wait for the Dragon to fight Mr. Doodle."

The fight between Mr. Doodle and the Dragon was a great sight to see. The Dragon could growl very loud when he wanted to and he growled louder than usual. But Mr. Doodle, even if he was so lazy that he wanted Marggy to chop his wood

for him, was very brave and every time the Dragon growled, Mr. Doodle stuck out his tongue at the Dragon.

This made the Dragon growl louder than ever and Raggedy Andy grew so excited he put a cream puff into his eye instead of his mouth and the cream puff covered his shoe button eye so that he could only watch the fight with one eye until Raggedy Ann wiped the cream puff off with her pocket hanky. The little white one with blue flowers on it.

Each time the Dragon rushed at Mr. Doodle and growled, Mr. Doodle jumped back. And each time Mr. Doodle rushed at the Dragon, the Dragon jumped back. And the fight lasted until both Mr. Doodle and the Dragon grew so excited, they forgot what they were doing, and both rushed at each other at the same time. This surprised the Dragon so much, he stopped suddenly and opened his mouth and he had no sooner done this than Mr. Doodle, who was as much surprised as the Dragon, lost his balance and fell right into the Dragon's mouth.

"Hm!" the Dragon said. "The great fight is over!"

"I'm glad that you swallowed Mr. Doodle instead of Mr. Doodle swallowing you!" Raggedy Andy told the Dragon as he patted him upon the head.

"Silly!" Raggedy Ann laughed at Raggedy Andy. "How could Mr. Doodle swallow the Dragon when the Dragon is so much larger?"

"I never thought of that," Raggedy Andy giggled. He knew when the joke was on him.

But suddenly the Dragon looked worried and it only took Raggedy Andy a moment to find out why. Mr. Doodle, inside the paper Dragon had started stomping around.

"If you don't let me out, I'll kick out all your slats!" Mr. Doodle shouted from inside the paper Dragon.

"I believe I had better let him out," the Dragon said. "I think he has nails in his shoes!"

So the Dragon opened his mouth and Mr. Doodle walked out. Mr. Doodle was so tired though, he had to sit down and rest. "We'll have another fight just as soon as I rest up a bit."

And because they did not believe in being stingy, Raggedy Ann and Raggedy Andy gave Mr. Doodle three cream puffs and six doughnuts to help him rest.

After resting and eating three cream puffs and six doughnuts, Mr. Doodle jumped to his feet. "Now we must continue our fight!" he cried to the Dragon.

"I won't fight you if you fall inside my mouth again and kick around like you did before. Your shoes have nails in them!" the Dragon said.

"I guess I'll take off my shoes then," Mr. Doodle agreed. "That will make it a fair fight, don't you think?"

When Mr. Doodle had taken off his shoes with the nails in the bottom the Dragon said, "I will never permit you to take Marggy home with you to chop your wood."

And Mr. Doodle replied, "And I will never permit you to not permit me to take Marggy home with me to chop my wood." And with this, Mr. Doodle stuck out his tongue at the Dragon and the Dragon growled very loud at Mr. Doodle. Then Mr. Doodle pushed upon the Dragon and the Dragon pushed upon Mr. Doodle and back and forth they tussled until finally the Dragon pushed the hardest and pushed Mr. Doodle over on his back.

Of course you have guessed by this time that Mr. Doodle was losing the fight with the Dragon, and it made him so angry he lost his temper, and before anyone could say, "Scat!" Mr. Doodle picked up a stone and threw it right smack dab through the kind Dragon's paper side.

"Aren't you ashamed of yourself, Mr. Doodle?" Raggedy Ann cried.

"I don't care," Mr. Doodle replied. "He shouldn't have pushed me over on my back, that's what!"

Marggy's Mama, before she stopped to think that Mr. Doodle did not belong to her, caught Mr. Doodle and turned him over her knee. And I wish that you could have heard the paddywhacks she gave him with her slipper. When Marggy's Mama had finished paddywacking Mr. Doodle, Mr. Doodle ran home as fast as he could.

"Ha! Ha! Ha!" the Dragon laughed in spite of the hole in his side, "Marggy's Mama is the one who really won the great fight!"

Raggedy Andy hunted around through the woods until he found a Sunday newspaper and with this and some of the cream from the cream puffs, Raggedy Andy and Raggedy Ann covered the hole in the paper Dragon's side. The Sunday newspaper was printed in colors and it made the paper Dragon much prettier than he had been and everyone told him so. And after they had thanked the kindly paper Dragon for rescuing Marggy from Mr. Doodle, they left the Dragon trying to wiggle around so that he could see the beautiful Sunday newspaper patch they had pasted on his side.

CHAPTER FIVE

"IT'S nice to go adventuring through the lovely woods!" Raggedy Ann said as they walked along.

"Yes, indeed it is," Marggy's Mama replied. "And wasn't it fortunate we met the kind paper Dragon! If it had not been for him, old Mr. Doodle would have taken Marggy home with him to chop his wood, and then we would not have been able to hunt any further for Marggy's Daddy."

"Dear me suz!" Raggedy Ann exclaimed as she looked back. "Here comes Mr. Doodle! Why doesn't he let us alone!"

"I'll get a nice long switch and we'll see about this!" Marggy's Mama said very severe-like, but when Mr. Doodle came running up, Marggy's Mama did not have to use the switch because Mr. Doodle had a box in his hands and said, "See what I found back in the woods!"

The box was made of shiny wood and on the front were black shiny knobs with little white numbers on them.

"What is it, Mr. Doodle?" Marggy's Mama asked, forgetting that she held the nice long switch.

"I do not know!" Mr. Doodle replied. "After I had the fight with the paper Dragon and after Marggy's Mama paddy-whacked me, I ran as fast as I could until I grew very tired; then I sat down to rest, and right in front of me in a hollow tree I saw this lovely box."

"I'll bet a nickel it is a magic box," Raggedy Andy said.

"Let's all sit down and maybe we can think what the box is for," Raggedy Ann suggested. So while they sat and thought, Marggy's Mama gave them each a cream puff, for everyone knows, you can think ever so much better while eating cream puffs.

Finally Raggedy Ann said, "I'll tell you what let's do!"

"What?" Mr. Doodle asked.

"All of you run over and hide in that hollow tree and I will open the box, then if a Magician, or a Genei hops out he won't know where you are."

"No sir!" Raggedy Andy said, very decidedly. "Mr. Doodle found the box and it belongs to him, so if there is a Magician, or a Genei in the magic box then Mr. Doodle can open it so that he will be caught instead of you, Raggedy Ann."

"That is true!" Mr. Doodle said. "I found the box and I tried to take Marggy home with me and caused you enough trouble, so you all run and hide and I will open the box!"

This was very kind of Mr. Doodle, for before he had been so very unkind to Marggy and her Mama and friends.

"Huh! I am not afraid," Raggedy Andy said. "I shall stand right here, and if a Magician or a Genei pops out of the box I will crack him on top of the head with this stubby stick."

"Indeed you shan't do that, Raggedy Andy," Raggedy Ann cried. "What if it should be a very kind hearted Magician, or a generous Genei who would help us find Marggy's Daddy? It wouldn't be nice to crack him on top of his head with the stubby stick!"

"Then I will not hit him on top of his head with the stick," Raggedy Andy agreed. "But just the same, I shall stay right here while Mr. Doodle opens the shiny box."

"Then we will all stay," Marggy's Mama said.

Mr. Doodle was just about to open the lid of the shiny box when Raggedy Ann cried, "Wait a moment! Before you open the box, try twisting the black knobs with the white numbers on them."

Everyone held their breaths while Mr. Doodle twisted the black knobs. "SQUEEEE—AWK—EEEE!"

"It sounds like you are pinching him when you twist the knobs!" Raggedy Andy said. Mr. Doodle twisted the knobs again and a voice from the box said, "Kay—dee—kay—aye," and then there came the tinkle of a piano.

"Someone lives in the box!" Raggedy Ann cried. "They are playing the piano."

"Yes! That's it, Raggedy Ann," Raggedy Andy said. "It is some little creature's home!"

"No it isn't!" a voice in back of Raggedy Ann said, and when they looked, our friends saw a little boy standing there and his eyes danced with merriment.

"How do you know?" Mr. Doodle asked.

"Because it is my box!" the boy replied, "I made it myself!"

"Then you must be a Magician, or a Fairy, or something!" Marggy's Mama said.

"Oh! Not at all," the little boy replied. "Almost any boy can make a box like that if he care to do so!"

"Well! It is my box now!" Mr. Doodle said as he picked up the shiny box and held it tightly under his arm.

"Why the idea, Mr. Doodle! It isn't your box at all!" Marggy's Mama cried.

"Yes it is!" Mr. Doodle shouted, "I found it in a hollow tree and so that makes it mine. Don't you see?"

"Why, Mr. Doodle! I'm s'prised at you!" Raggedy Ann said. "The pretty shiny box belongs to the nice little boy and you must give it to him!"

"I'll run with it and then you can't catch me!" Mr. Doodle said as he started running. The little boy ran after Mr. Doodle and so did Raggedy Andy.

The little boy could not run as fast as Raggedy Andy, so Raggedy Andy caught hold of Mr. Doodle's coat tails and held him. Mr. Doodle pulled and pulled until one of his coat tails came off and let Raggedy Andy fall down.

"Now then you'll catch it, Raggedy Andy!" Mr. Doodle screamed. "I shall pull off your coat tail because you pulled off my coat tail!" And he jumped at Raggedy Andy.

"Ha, ha, ha, ha! I haven't any coat tails!"

"Then we will have to fight!" Mr. Doodle cried.

"All right!" and Raggedy Andy rolled up his sleeves.

Mr. Doodle and Raggedy Andy were just about to fight when Raggedy Ann came running up. "Here!" she cried, "You mustn't fight! It isn't nice to quarrel and fight like cats and dogs! Besides, the little boy has taken the shiny box and run home with it."

"It was really all my fault," Mr. Doodle said when Raggedy Andy said he was sorry he tore his coat. "If I had not been so selfish and had not tried to run away with the little boy's shiny box you would not have torn my coat even a speck!"

"What kind of a magic box do you think it really was, Mr. Doodle?" Raggedy Ann wished to know.

"It was a radio," Mr. Doodle replied. "Didn't you guess that? Almost any one would guess it the first pop!"

"We had better hurry on so that we can find Marggy's Daddy," said Raggedy Ann. "You know he has been lost for the longest, longest time."

"When you hunt for Marggy's Daddy, why don't you have Marggy stay at my house?" Mr. Doodle asked. "She will get tired walking so far with you."

"Now, Mr. Doodle!" Raggedy Ann shook her rag thumb at him. "You know very well that Marggy wants to go with us and you just want her to go home with you so that she will chop the wood and build the fires 'n everything; 'cause you are too lazy to do it yourself!"

"Whoever says I am lazy will have to fight like the paper Dragon and I fought," Mr. Doodle cried as he hopped to his feet.

Raggedy Andy did not want Mr. Doodle to fight Raggedy Ann so he started rolling up his sleeves to fight Mr. Doodle in Raggedy Ann's place when Mrs. Doodle came running up from behind the tree and took Mr. Doodle right by his ear.

"Now then, Mr. Doodle," she cried as she pulled him along, "You march right home with me! I'm tired of having you try to get someone else to do the work all the time. From now on, you must do it yourself, you lazy thing."

And Mrs. Doodle meant just what she said too, for as long as they watched, Mrs. Doodle still had hold of Mr. Doodle's ear and was making him step towards home as fast as he could go without falling down.

CHAPTER SIX

FINALLY our friends came to a great stone castle with large gates in front of it. At one side of the gate was a great big soldier with a long gun and at the other side of the gate was a great big soldier with a long sword. "You can't come through the gate!" the two soldiers shouted when they saw our friends.

"If you walk through the gate, I'll have to cut off your ears!" the soldier with the long sword cried.

"I haven't any ears," Raggedy Andy laughed.

"Besides, the gate doesn't open anyway," the soldier with the gun said.

"If they won't let us go through the gate, let's walk around it," Raggedy Ann said.

"There!" one soldier said to the other. "I knew they'd guess it!"

"How did you ever think to walk around the gate when you couldn't walk through it?" one soldier asked.

"Because there isn't any fence on the sides of the gate!" Raggedy Ann laughed. Then the door opened and all walked right into the castle.

When Raggedy Ann, who came last had entered the castle, the great door closed behind her. Then the rug they were standing upon tipped down, so that Raggedy Andy, Marggy

and her Mama and Raggedy Ann all went scooting down a
slippery slide. Down, down they went, ever so fast, under the
castle and when they came to the end, there they were on the
road with the castle in back of them.

"I'm glad we didn't have to stay in the castle," Raggedy
Andy said. "For who knows? It might have been a magical
castle and we might have had to stay there for ever and ever!"

At the side of the road sat an old man. He sat upon
a hard stone and he was knitting sox. After they had all
said, "Good morning" to the old man, Marggy's Mama
asked him, "Is this a magician's castle?"

"Yes, indeed it is!" the old man replied. "I'm trying my best to get in, for the Magician has a very magical canary bird of mine which sings beautiful songs all day long."

"Maybe you can climb up the slippery slide."

"No, I can't do that!" the old man said. "For you see, the slippery slide is too steep and slippery. I'll tell you a secret though, if you promise not to tell anyone."

"We promise!" Marggy said.

"Well, the secret is this," the old man whispered. "I'm knitting sixteen pair of sox and when I have them finished I shall unravel them and tie a stone to one end of the yarn. Then I'll throw the stone up to one of the windows and the stone will go behind one of the iron bars in front of the window and bounce out again. Then I will let the stone pull the yarn down until it touches the ground. I'll tie a rope to the yarn and pull the rope up to the window, then I'll climb up there and get in. Isn't that a nice secret? Do not tell anyone!"

"Oh, no, we won't," Raggedy Ann said. "But," she added, "have you thought that if you used the yarn before you knitted it into sox, you wouldn't have the trouble of unraveling it?"

"Dear me, no! I never thought of that!" the old man replied. "I've been sitting here for nine months knitting the sox and I am on the last one!"

"And then, too," Raggedy Ann wanted to know. "Even if you climbed up to the window, how would you get through the iron bars?"

"I am afraid I did not think of that either!" the old man sighed.

"And have you thought that maybe you can walk right into the front door if you go around there?" Raggedy Andy asked.

"No sir! I never thought of that either!"

"Have you thought of eating since you started knitting the sox?" Marggy's Mama asked.

"Dear me! I've been so busy, I forgot that too!"

"Then I'll tell you what I would do if I were you," Marggy's Mama said as she gave the old man eight cream puffs and nine doughnuts. "I'd eat these, then I'd run home to my mama as fast as I could scamper."

"Oh, thank you!" the old man chuckled. "I'll run home to mama right away. I'd forgotten her. Maybe she will be hungry too." And away he went, lickity split through the woods.

"Well, well, well!" Raggedy Ann laughed as she watched the funny old man run away. "He has gone and left the sox he has been working on so long!"

Marggy's Mama picked up the sox and put them in her basket. "If we pass his house I will hand them to him."

"Here he comes running back!" Marggy cried. "Isn't he funny?"

"Hello!" he cried as he came up to our friends. "Do you know where I was running to? I was running as hard as I could through the woods when all of a sudden I wondered what I was running for. So I came back to ask you!"

"You were taking the doughnuts and cream puffs home to give to your mama," Marggy's Mama explained.

"Oh! So I was!" the funny old man said. "Well sir, I have eaten all the doughnuts and cream puffs!"

"That is too bad!" Raggedy Ann said. "For you told us your mama might be very hungry while you had been away nine months knitting the sox!"

"Dear me! So I did!" the old man admitted. "I must hurry back and get the sox and then hurry right home before I forget it!"

"Wait a moment!" Raggedy Ann cried as the funny old

man started to run, "Marggy's Mama has your sox in her basket, so you will not have to run back!"

"Then I must run home as fast as I can and see how my mama is, she may be very hungry."

"Now we will hurry after him and see where his home is for if he has been away for nine months, his mama will be very, very hungry and will like our doughnuts and cream puffs," Raggedy Ann said thoughtfully.

Raggedy Ann and Raggedy Andy and Marggy and her Mama caught hold of hands and ran after the funny little man until they saw him run into a queer little house. Smoke was coming out of the chimney and when they walked up to the door a nice little old lady came to meet them. "Come right in!" she cried cheerily. "My husband told me you might be along pretty soon, and as I have been making some candy covered cup cakes, I would like you to come in and have some with lemonade." And she took Raggedy Ann and her friends into the dining room and gave them all they could eat and drink. When they had finished, the funny old man's wife asked, "Why has Mr. Felix got that piece of red yarn tied around his nose?"

Raggedy Ann laughed. "Why! Mrs. Felix, hasn't he told you?"

"No!" Mrs. Felix replied. "He had forgotten by the time he reached home!"

"Then I'll tell you why he has it tied around his nose," Raggedy Ann said. "We met him back by the castle and gave him some cream puffs and doughnuts to bring home to you, for he told us he had not been home for nine months. You see, we thought you might be hungry, so we tied the yarn around his nose so he wouldn't forget to run right straight home!"

"Dear me!" Mrs. Felix sighed, "I do not know what to do for Mr. Felix. He forgets everything. Why just an hour ago I sent him down to the grocery to get a loaf of bread and a pound of bacon and you found him sitting along the road. I guess he forgot that I sent him to the store!"

"No! I didn't forget to go to the store," Mr. Felix said. "But I forgot what you sent me for, so I bought fifteen pairs of sox and some yarn and knitting needles."

"And he told us he was knitting the sox himself!" Marggy said.

"Dear me, what can I do with him?" Mrs. Felix cried. "When he was a little boy he used to tell fibs and as an excuse for telling fibs he would say, 'I forgot' until he told it so many times he finally got so he really did forget, and now he cannot remember anything!"

"My goodness!" Raggedy Ann said, "I am glad there are not many children like him; for think how queer it would be to have them grow up and not be able to remember anything!"

"Maybe you can cure him of forgetting by making him go without his supper and see if he is hungry enough in the morning to remember it. Then if he forgets, make him go without his dinner and see if he forgets that!" Marggy said.

"Oh my! He would never forget anything like that!" Mrs. Felix laughed. "It's just the other things he forgets."

"Then I believe a good paddywhacking would be the best thing for him," Raggedy Ann laughed.

"Just the thing!" Mrs. Felix cried as she seized the pancake paddle and before he had time to run, Mr. Felix found himself across Mrs. Felix's knees and was being paddywhacked real hard.

"Now will you remember not to forget?" Mrs. Felix asked.

"Indeed I will!" Mr. Felix replied as he wiped his forehead with his pocket hanky, and to prove that he remembered not to forget, Mr. Felix repeated every single thing he had told Raggedy Ann back near the castle in the woods.

"I'll bet a nickel I never, never forget again," Mr. Felix said. "Never, never, for it isn't any fun being paddywhacked with a pancake paddle, I can tell you!"

"We asked Mr. Felix who lived in the castle and he told us a Magician lived there," Raggedy Ann said.

"Yes, that is true," Mrs. Felix said. "Didn't you run in to see him when you passed?"

"We went in," Raggedy Andy laughed, "But we hardly stepped inside the door before we slid down a slippery slide and went scooting out on this side!"

"Then if the Magician is a kindly Magician, what do you say if we go to see him? He may be able to tell us where Marggy's Daddy is," Raggedy Ann said.

Marggy and her Mama thought this would be a good plan. "And," Marggy's Mama said. "Even if we should slide down the slippery slide again, it is a lot of fun!"

So thanking Mrs. Felix for the nice cup cakes and lemonade, our friends returned to the gate where the two soldiers stood guard.

"Hello!" Raggedy Ann cried in her cheeriest voice. "We wish to go in and visit the Magician."

"Alright!" one of the soldiers said. "But you will have to walk around the gate, because you know it doesn't open!"

"Thank you!" Raggedy Ann said. "When we went in the door before, we dropped through the floor and went scooting down a slippery slide, way under the castle!"

One of the soldiers came up to Raggedy Ann and whispered, "Don't tell a soul, Raggedy Ann!" he said. "It's a secret. When you go in the castle, you must go around to the side door. Everyone who goes in the front door, falls down and scoots on the slippery slide!"

"Did you ever see Marggy's Daddy walking along here?" Raggedy Andy asked one of the soldiers.

"I don't believe so," the soldier replied. "But when you go inside, you ask the Magician. He knows ever and ever so much!"

So the Raggedys thanked the kind soldiers and walking around to the side door rang a little bell. In answer to the bell, the door was opened a crack and a long nose was poked out. "Who is it?" the owner of the long nose asked.

Raggedy Ann named over all in the little party, then said, "We wish to ask the Magician if he knows where Marggy's Daddy is, her Daddy has been lost a long, long time."

"Wait a moment!" the long nosed person said. "I will run and ask the Magician!"

Presently the long nosed man returned. "The Magician says that he knows where Marggy's Daddy is, but he will not tell unless you do something for him!"

"What does he wish us to do for him?" Raggedy Andy wanted to know.

"The Magician will tell you!" the long nosed man said as he opened the door and they followed him down a long hall.

In a large room, sitting upon a throne was a queer little man with long whiskers. This was the Magician who owned the castle. He greeted our friends by tipping his crown. "Hello!" he said. "If you want to find Marggy's Daddy, you must do something for me first! That's the way they always do things in fairy tales."

"But this isn't a fairy tale," Raggedy Ann said.

"Of course it is!" the magician laughed. "How can two rag dolls walk and talk unless it is a fairy tale. So I want you to go out and bring me back a dragon, then maybe I can think of something else for you to do!"

Raggedy Ann and Raggedy Andy whispered together, then Raggedy Andy asked, "If I bring you a dragon, what will you do with him?"

"I do not know," the Magician answered. "I never had a dragon, but I've read of them in fairy tales and every great Magician really needs a dragon around his castle. I 'spect though, I would have to keep him in a chicken coop to keep him from eating people!"

"I believe I can bring you a dragon," Raggedy Andy said. "But it will be a very nice, kind Dragon who does not eat people, so if you will promise that you won't put him in a cage, but let him live here in the castle with you until he gets ready to leave, I will go and hunt for him."

"All right," the Magician promised.

So Raggedy Andy filled his pockets with doughnuts from Marggy's Mama's basket and started out the door.

"Wait a moment!" the Magician cried. "You mustn't go to fight a Dragon without a sword." And he handed Raggedy Andy a wooden sword.

"Do you really believe Raggedy Andy will bring back a Dragon?" the Magician asked as he motioned Raggedy Ann and Marggy and her Mama to take seats near him.

"I wouldn't be a bit surprised if he brought back a nice fat Dragon," Raggedy Ann laughed and winked one of her shoe button eyes at Marggy's Mama. Then the Magician clapped his hands and two servants came in with trays of ice cream sodas.

When Raggedy Andy left Raggedy Ann and Marggy and her Mama at the castle of the Magician, he ran with his wooden sword through the woods back to where they left the paper Dragon. "Yoo hoo!" Raggedy Andy called in his loudest Raggedy voice. But call as loud as he could, the paper Dragon did not reply.

"That's funny," Raggedy Andy cried. "I wonder what has become of the Dragon?"

"I'll tell you where the paper Dragon is," a little Gnome said as he walked up to Raggedy Andy. "After you left, Mr. Doodle came and dragged the paper Dragon home."

"Dear me," Raggedy Andy sighed. "Now we shall never be able to find Marggy's Daddy."

"I'm afraid not!" the little Gnome said. "For I heard Mr. Doodle tell Mrs. Doodle that he would make a chicken coop out of the Dragon."

"If Mr. Doodle has broken up that lovely, kindly, paper Dragon to make a chicken coop, I don't know what I shall do to Mr. Doodle," promised Raggedy Andy.

"Then maybe you had better hurry to Mr. Doodle's house as soon as you can," advised the little Gnome. "If that sword was given you by the Magician," the little Gnome added, "It must be a magic sword, so get on it just like you would a hobby horse and see if it doesn't carry you along faster than you can run on your cotton stuffed legs."

Raggedy Andy was greatly surprised, but when he straddled the magic wooden sword and held his feet off the ground, the wooden sword went sailing along above the ground a lot faster than Raggedy Andy could run. And while the wooden sword carried him along toward Mr. Doodle's house, Raggedy Andy ate the doughnuts he had brought along, because he knew if he had to fight Mr. Doodle he would need lots of strength. And of course doughnuts are very good to give you strength, if you do not eat too many of them.

Raggedy Andy felt sure he could coax the kind paper Dragon to return with him to the Magician's castle.

The magic sword soon carried Raggedy Andy right to Mr. Doodle's front door.

Raggedy Andy took the wooden sword and knocked on Mr. Doodle's front door. Bang! Bang! Bang! But no one answered. So Raggedy Andy walked out in back of the fence and there was Mr. and Mrs. Doodle and the paper Dragon.

Mr. Doodle had tied the paper Dragon to stakes and was trying to drive all his chickens in the paper Dragon's mouth, but the chickens did not care to go in the paper Dragon, because they thought the Dragon would eat them, and the paper Dragon did not wish the chickens inside his paper body any more than the chickens wanted to be there, so the paper Dragon tried his best to growl and frighten the chickens. Mr. Doodle had put a stick in the paper Dragon's mouth and this kept the Dragon from growling as loud as Dragons usually growl.

Mrs. Doodle shooed the chickens and Mr. Doodle shooed the chickens and the paper Dragon did not like it even a teeny weeny bit, so you bet he was very glad when Raggedy Andy walked up and asked in a loud stern voice, "What are you doing with that Dragon, Mr. Doodle?"

"I'm making a chicken coop out of the Dragon, that's what!" Mr. Doodle replied.

"And I've come to rescue the Dragon, that's what, Mr. Doodle!" Raggedy Andy said.

"But I shan't let you rescue him!" Mr. Doodle shouted quite loud.

"And I say, I SHALL RESCUE HIM!" Raggedy Andy shouted still louder.

Neither one knew what to do next until Mrs. Doodle went in the house and brought out tea and cinnamon toast. "I will think of a way to fight pretty soon," Mr. Doodle promised as he passed the tea and toast to Raggedy Andy.

After they had finished eating and had wiped the cinnamon from around their mouths, Raggedy Andy knew it was time to rescue the Dragon, so he said to Mr. Doodle, "Maybe you

don't know it, but this wooden sword I carry is a very magical wooden sword. The Magician gave it to me, so that I could bring the Dragon to his castle. Now if I should crack you on top of your head with the sword, it will make a large bump and you will not be able to wear your hat, it will hurt so much."

"Then maybe I had better let you rescue the Dragon," said Mr. Doodle.

"I believe that will be the best way to do," Raggedy Andy replied. "And anyway the chickens do not care to go inside a Dragon chicken coop."

"Indeed, that is true," Mr. Doodle agreed. So Raggedy Andy cut all the ropes which held the paper Dragon, and the paper Dragon was so thankful, he wiggled all over and would have licked Raggedy Andy's hand, only whoever made the paper Dragon, forgot to make him a paper tongue, so he couldn't even lick a postage stamp.

"We'd better be going," Raggedy Andy told the Dragon. "The Magician wished me to bring you to the castle."

"I'd rather be a chicken coop than have the Magician shut me up in a cage," Mr. Doodle teased.

"Don't pay any attention to him," Raggedy Andy whispered. "He's just peevish because I rescued you."

"I know it," the Dragon laughed. "And even if the Magician shuts me up in a cage, I'll go with you anyway, because I shall be very glad to help you find Marggy's Daddy."

Raggedy Andy and the paper Dragon went through the woods towards the Magician's castle. "It won't be very long until we get there," said Raggedy Andy.

"Maybe if you would ride upon my head, we could go a little faster," the Dragon suggested. So Raggedy Andy climbed upon the Dragon's head and the Dragon wiggled through the woods, lickety split. The paper Dragon was very long; his head was very far in front of his tail, and so when the Dragon suddenly stopped, Raggedy Andy flew right off the Dragon's head and lit upon the soft ground.

"Why did you stop?" Raggedy Andy asked.

"I believe my tail is fastened on a stick," the Dragon replied.

Raggedy Andy could not see whether the Dragon's tail was fastened on a stick or not, so he ran back to look.

"Ha! Ha! Ha! That's the time I fooled you!" cried Mr. Doodle.

Yes, sir, it was him! He had run after Raggedy Andy and the Dragon and now, there he sat upon a stone and laughed.

"Why did you fasten the Dragon's tail on a stick?" Raggedy Andy asked.

"I didn't fasten his tail to a stick!" shouted Mr. Doodle. "I want the paper Dragon for a chicken coop, so I put salt on his tail!"

"Dear me! that was very unkind of you!" Raggedy Andy cried, for you see he knew very well that the way to catch Dragons is to put salt upon their tails.

But it isn't nice to have someone else put salt upon a Dragon's tail when that Dragon is a nice friendly Dragon, for a Dragon can't even wiggle a smidgin when it has salt upon its tail. Raggedy Andy sat down beside Mr. Doodle and tried to think of a way to rescue the Dragon again. And while he sat there and thought, he nibbled on one of his doughnuts, and seeing that Mr. Doodle looked hungry, Raggedy Andy gave

Mr. Doodle a doughnut too. For, it is best to be generous and unselfish, even to those who are unkind to us.

"If I don't take the Dragon to the Magician's castle, the Magician will not tell us where Marggy's Daddy is," Raggedy Andy told Mr. Doodle.

"I know it," Mr. Doodle replied as he nibbled the doughnut. "But if you take the Dragon to the Magician's castle, then don't you see, I shall be unable to make the paper Dragon into a chicken coop."

"The paper Dragon will not make a very good chicken coop," Raggedy Andy said.

"Cause why?" Mr. Doodle wanted to know.

"Because," Raggedy Andy explained. "Some time when the chickens are walking into the paper Dragon's mouth, the paper Dragon will bite them."

"Ha, ha, ha!" Mr. Doodle laughed. "I'll prop the Dragon's mouth open with a long stick, so that he won't bite the chickens."

"If you do that, Mr. Doodle, all the chickens will walk right out of his mouth, cause it will always be open."

But just as Raggedy Andy and Mr. Doodle finished eating their doughnuts Raggedy Andy had an idea. "When Mr. Doodle put salt upon the Dragon's tail, the Dragon could not move," he thought to himself. "So if I want to rescue the nice Dragon, I must brush the salt off his tail!"

So Raggedy Andy said to Mr. Doodle, "How much salt did you put on the Dragon's tail, Mr. Doodle?"

"You can see how much," Mr. Doodle replied as he pointed to the pile of salt on the Dragon's tail.

"Why didn't you put more on his tail?"

"Because that is all the salt I had with me!"

This was what Raggedy Andy wanted to know for Raggedy Andy knew if he brushed the salt off the Dragon's tail, the Dragon would be able to wiggle away through the woods.

"You stay here and eat this doughnut," Raggedy Andy said to Mr. Doodle. "While I go up to the Dragon's head and see if he feels all right."

"Do not stay too long," Mr. Doodle said. "For just as soon as I eat this doughnut, I shall take the Dragon home."

So Raggedy Andy ran up to the Dragon's head and said to him, "Now if I can, I shall fool Mr. Doodle and brush all the salt off your tail. So as soon as you feel all the salt brushed off, you must wiggle through the woods to the Magician's castle just as fast as you can wiggle, and I will hop upon the magic wooden sword the Magician gave me and we will escape from Mr. Doodle."

The paper Dragon promised that he would wiggle as fast as he had ever wiggled before, so Raggedy Andy walked back to Mr. Doodle at the Dragon's tail.

"So you think that you can fool me some way and brush the salt off the Dragon's tail, do you?" Mr. Doodle asked when Raggedy Andy came up.

"How in the world did you guess it?" Raggedy Andy asked.

Mr. Doodle laughed. "When you talked to the paper Dragon's head, I listened at his tail, and because the paper Dragon is hollow all the way down I could hear just as plain as if you talked through a pipe."

"Then I guess there is no way for me to fool you, Mr. Doodle," Raggedy Andy said in a sad voice.

"You can't fool me very easy, that is sure," Mr. Doodle replied as he brushed the doughnut crumbs away from his mouth.

"Did you ever see a hippopotamus up in a tree, Mr. Doodle?" Raggedy Andy asked as he looked up in the tree above him.

"No! I never did, Raggedy Andy! And what's more, I never will see a hippopotamus up in a tree!" Mr. Doodle replied.

"And that is true, Mr. Doodle, if you never look up in trees," Raggedy Andy said. "For how can you expect to see a hippopotamus up in a tree, if you do not look?" And as Mr. Doodle was very anxious to see a hippopotamus up a tree, he looked up.

"I don't see him at all," he said.

"Neither do I, Mr. Doodle." And as he said this, Raggedy Andy reached over and brushed every speck of salt off the Dragon's tail, and away went the paper Dragon through the woods towards the Magician's castle as fast as he could wiggle. When Raggedy Andy jumped upon the magic wooden sword and told the magic wooden sword to follow the paper Dragon, the magic wooden sword did not budge a speck.

"Ha! Ha! Ha!" Mr. Doodle laughed when Raggedy Andy looked surprised. "The magic wooden sword will not carry you away, because I tied a string to the wooden sword and to that stump!"

"If I only had a knife, I would cut the string!" Raggedy Andy laughed although he felt very disappointed.

"Now you have made me lose the paper Dragon," Mr. Doodle said. "So instead of making a chicken coop out of the paper Dragon, as I wished to do, I shall take you home and make you build me a chicken coop out of boards!"

Raggedy Andy did not know what else to say, so he said to Mr. Doodle, "I don't believe I can go back to your house and build a chicken coop today, because I'm too busy."

But Mr. Doodle only laughed real loud. "It won't do any good for you to tell me you are too busy today to build me a chicken coop!" Mr. Doodle cried as he dragged Raggedy Andy home and tied him with a string near the wood pile. "Now while I go in the house and eat my dinner, you can start building the chicken coop." And he gave Raggedy Andy a saw and a hammer and a lot of nails. "And if you don't have the chicken coop finished when I get through my dinner I shall paddywhack you," Mr. Doodle promised.

So Raggedy Andy sawed the boards and nailed them together. Then he happened to think, "I can saw the string in two and run to where Mr. Doodle has the wooden sword tied to the stump and saw the string which holds the magic wooden sword." Raggedy Andy had just finished sawing the string with which Mr. Doodle had tied him, when Mr. Doodle came running out of his house.

"That's the time I fooled you!" Raggedy Andy cried as he ran with the saw through the woods. When he came to where the magic wooden sword was tied to the stump, Raggedy Andy cut the strings. And just as Mr. Doodle ran up to catch him, Raggedy Andy jumped on the magic sword and cried, "Magic wooden sword, carry me after the paper Dragon to the Magician's castle!" And the magic wooden sword flew over the ground so fast Mr. Doodle was left far behind.

CHAPTER SEVEN

R AGGEDY Andy soon reached the large gate in front of the Magician's castle. There stood the two soldiers; one with a real long sword and the other with a real long gun and they held up their hands and cried, "Stop!"

"Did you see a Dragon come by this way?" Raggedy Andy asked the two soldiers.

"Yes!" the soldiers replied. "The Dragon frightened us so we ran and hid and the Dragon climbed right up to the window and wiggled in the castle. Maybe by this time the Dragon has eaten the Magician."

"I shall go inside and see!" Raggedy Andy replied.

But the two soldiers said, "We will not let you go inside the castle and be eaten by the Dragon!"

But Raggedy Andy looked back and saw that Mr. Doodle was running after him as hard as he could come, so Raggedy Andy just whispered to the magic wooden sword and the magic wooden sword carried Raggedy Andy right over the two soldiers' heads and over the gate, just as Mr. Doodle came running up.

"Catch him!" Mr. Doodle cried, but of course he was too late. The wooden sword carried Raggedy Andy right to the castle door, but the door was locked and Raggedy Andy could not get in.

Mr. Doodle kicked so much, the two soldiers could not hold him so just as Mr. Doodle came running up, Raggedy Andy cried to the wooden sword, "Get up, wooden sword, fly up through the window in the castle!"

Once inside the Magician's castle, Raggedy Andy went down stairs to the room where the Magician usually sat upon his throne. But everything was topsy turvy. The chairs were turned over and the Magician's throne was upside down.

"Dear me!" Raggedy Andy exclaimed as he ran his rag hand up through his red yarn hair, "I wonder what could have happened?" So Raggedy Andy went all through the castle until he found the Dragon.

"Well!" said Raggedy Andy, "I'm glad that I found you. I had a hard time escaping from Mr. Doodle. He dragged me home and made me start building his chicken coop, but while he was eating his dinner, I sawed the string with which he had tied me and escaped."

The Dragon only looked at Raggedy Andy in a funny way, but did not say anything.

"Have you seen the Magician and Raggedy Ann and Marggy and her Mama?" Raggedy Andy asked the Dragon.

"Mumble, mumble, mumble," was all the Dragon replied, for he was trying to talk without opening his mouth.

"Now!" Raggedy Andy said as he pointed his rag thumb at the Dragon. "Tell me! Did you swallow the Magician?"

The Dragon nodded his head up and down and Raggedy Andy knew then that the Dragon had swallowed them.

"Open your mouth!" Raggedy Andy told the Dragon. So the Dragon opened his mouth and the Magician and Raggedy Ann and Marggy and her Mama came walking out.

"You must leave my castle right away!" the Magician
cried. "I won't have a Dragon around here swallowing people
like this Dragon did."

"But he is only a paper Dragon, Mr. Magician!"

"I know he is now!" the Magician replied. "But how was
I to know he was made out of paper when he came wiggling
through the window and swallowed all of us?"

"Why did you swallow them?" Raggedy Andy asked the
Dragon.

"I did not know what to do until you came," the Dragon replied. "So I just swallowed everybody and waited until you came."

"And now you must take the Dragon and leave!" the
Magician cried and pushed them all outside.

"Oh, dear!" Raggedy Andy cried. "Now that the Dragon
has made the Magician so peevish, he will never tell us where
Marggy's Daddy is and we shall never find him. And, besides,
Mr. Doodle is out here fighting with the two soldiers and if
he wins the fight, he will capture the Dragon and we will have
to rescue the Dragon all over again!"

"Let us hurry away while Mr. Doodle and the two soldiers
are still fighting," Raggedy Ann suggested. "Perhaps Mr.
Doodle will not see us!" So they all started to run. But
Mr. Doodle, just as soon as he caught sight of the Dragon and
Raggedy Ann and Andy trying to escape, quit fighting with
the two soldiers and ran after our friends, and because Marggy

and her Mama could not run very fast Mr. Doodle soon caught the Dragon's tail and stopped him. Mr. Doodle started to drag the Dragon towards his house, but Raggedy Ann and Raggedy Andy and Marggy and her Mama caught hold of the Dragon's head and pulled the other way.

Mr. Doodle pulled and pulled and our friends pulled and pulled until they all pulled so hard, the paper Dragon tore right in two. And Mr. Doodle was pulling so hard and our friends were pulling so hard, when the paper Dragon was torn in two, they all fell over backwards.

"Now then you have done it, Mr. Doodle," Raggedy Ann cried as she jumped to her feet and ran back to Mr. Doodle. "Aren't you ashamed of yourself?"

"No I am not!" Mr. Doodle replied. "If you had not pulled upon the Dragon's head, he would not have torn in two!"

Raggedy Andy took the Dragon's tail away from Mr. Doodle. "I have a good mind to box your ears, Mr. Doodle!" Raggedy Andy said.

"Ha! Ha! Ha!" Mr. Doodle laughed. "Your hands are made of cloth and stuffed with cotton, so it wouldn't hurt if you did!"

"Then I shall try mine!" Marggy's Mama cried. And if Raggedy Ann had not stopped her, Marggy's Mama would have given Mr. Doodle a box on the ear which he would have remembered for a long time.

The paper Dragon looked very sad, for he could not wiggle at all with his tail torn off and he wished to go with our friends on their journey in search of Marggy's Daddy. And then, too, when the paper Dragon was torn in two, that let the air whistle right through his paper body each time he opened his mouth. Marggy's Mama would have liked to paddywhack Mr. Doodle, but she knew that would do no good. "We must fix the paper Dragon together some way," she said.

Raggedy Ann had mended a hole in the paper Dragon's side once before with the cream from a cream puff and a pretty colored Sunday newspaper, but now they only had

chocolate cake, doughnuts and cookies left, for they had eaten all the cream puffs. Raggedy Andy suggested that by using little sticks as pins, they might pin the Dragon's tail together. "Of course he will still be torn!" Raggedy Andy said, "but if we can fix him together so that he can travel with us, maybe along the way, we will find a way to glue him together!"

So they all gathered little twigs and with these they pinned the Dragon's tail to the front part of his body. Even Mr. Doodle helped. Raggedy Ann and Raggedy Andy did not care to have Mr. Doodle go with them in search of Marggy's Daddy, nor did they wish him to take the Dragon back home for a chicken coop, but they were too polite to tell him so.

"It is too bad Mr. Doodle tore the tail from the paper Dragon," Raggedy Ann said, " 'cause now the paper Dragon can not wiggle along very fast."

"I'm glad he can't wiggle along very fast," Mr. Doodle laughed. "For I will follow you and just as soon as you find someone to mend the Dragon, I will take him away from you and use him for a chicken coop."

Raggedy Andy did not reply to Mr. Doodle but he thought, "When we have the nice paper Dragon mended, I will not let you take him away from us!"

So the Dragon wiggled along very slowly so as not to unfasten his tail and Raggedy Ann and Raggedy Andy and Marggy and her Mama walked beside him. Although they did not want him with them, Mr. Doodle went along. After a while they came to a funny little house. There was only one room down stairs and all the other rooms were built right on top of each other.

CHAPTER EIGHT

"WE will go inside and get something to eat," Mr. Doodle said. "I pulled so hard on the Dragon's tail, I am hungry." And without even knocking on the door, Mr. Doodle walked right inside the funny little house.

"You should not walk into any one's house without knocking, Mr. Doodle," Raggedy Ann told him.

But Mr. Doodle only laughed, "Ha! ha, ha!" like that, only a great deal louder, and went in anyway.

"Now that he is inside, we have a good chance to run away from him!" Raggedy Andy said.

The others thought this would be a good plan because Mr. Doodle had always been so mean to them, but when they heard Mr. Doodle squealing ever so loudly, they waited to see what was happening. My goodness! Didn't Mr. Doodle squeal? He squealed so loud and so long, Raggedy Andy said, "I 'spect I had better go inside and see why Mr. Doodle squeals!" Raggedy Andy was very polite, so he knocked upon the door.

"Come in!" someone said in a cheery voice, so Raggedy Andy walked in and saw Mr. Doodle standing with his long nose caught in a cupboard door and there stood a little man watching Mr. Doodle.

"Do you know," the little man said, "Mr. Doodle walked right into my house without knocking and poked his nose in my cupboard; and the cupboard door flew shut and caught him. It serves him right for snooping in other people's things!"

"Indeed it does!" Raggedy Andy agreed. "But Mr. Doodle is squealing so loud, maybe it would be best to open the cupboard door so that he can pull his nose out."

So the little man opened the cupboard door and Mr. Doodle sat down upon the floor and held his nose.

"Now all of you come inside," the little man said to Raggedy Ann and Marggy and her Mama. "And we will have something to eat, for I know you must all be hungry!" So he gave them chocolate cake and cookies and ice cream and dill pickles and milk and it was a very nice dinner. Mr. Doodle's nose hurt so much he could not eat anything and he was very sorry that he had not knocked upon the door instead of walking in and snooping around.

The little man filled Marggy's Mama's basket with lots of good things to eat, "So you will not get hungry along the way," he said, then turning to Mr. Doodle the little man said, "Mr. Doodle, if I were you, I would run right straight home—Raggedy Ann and Raggedy Andy and Marggy and her Mama do not care to have you go with them. Besides, you are so ill mannered you will always be getting into trouble. You had better run home, I believe your Mama is calling you."

"I shall not go home until I get the Dragon!" Mr. Doodle shouted, much louder than was necessary. "Because why? Because I intend making him into a chicken coop!"

"Mr. Doodle pulled the nice tail off of the kind paper Dragon," Raggedy Ann told the little man. "We had to mend his tail with little sticks."

"Yes!" Mr. Doodle cried. "And as soon as we get some glue to mend the Dragon's tail, I shall take the Dragon away from Raggedy Ann and Raggedy Andy!"

"I will give Raggedy Andy some glue," the little man said. "And sometime when Mr. Doodle is asleep, Raggedy Andy can mend the Dragon's tail and all get upon the Dragon's back and escape from Mr. Doodle."

Raggedy Andy put the bottle of glue in his pocket and then the little man took everyone except Mr. Doodle up to the top room. Mr. Doodle wanted to go with them, but the little man said, "No sir, Mr. Doodle, you must stay down stairs while we look out over the woods and see if we can see Marggy's Daddy."

So Mr. Doodle had to sit downstairs and twiddle his thumbs while the others went up and looked out over the deep, deep woods.

"Did Marggy's Daddy have four fingers and a thumb upon each hand?" the little man asked as they looked out the window.

"Yes!" Marggy's Mama said.

"And did he have two eyes and one nose and one mouth and two ears and hair on top of his head and two feet?" the little man asked.

"Yes!" Marggy's Mama replied.

"Then," said the little man, "I'll bet a nickel your Daddy was here, for a man who answered his description came here and asked for something to eat yesterday."

The little man told them the direction Marggy's Daddy had gone, so they thanked him and went downstairs.

"Oh, dear me!" Raggedy Ann cried when she walked out the door. "Mr. Doodle has gone and he has taken the Dragon with him!"

"Well! We must run after him and take the Dragon away from him!" Raggedy Andy said.

So Raggedy Ann and Raggedy Andy and Marggy and her Mama ran after Mr. Doodle until they came up to him.

"Now!" cried Raggedy Ann, as she stamped her rag foot. "Why did you take the Dragon away from us, Mr. Doodle? Just you tell me that!"

"Because I wish to make a chicken coop out of him! That's what and I shall not tell you again, Miss Raggedy Ann, and besides, I grew tired waiting for you back in the funny little house! I know that I can mend the Dragon's tail with glue a whole lot better than Raggedy Andy can, and I shall do it as soon as I get home!"

"You know perfectly well, Mr. Doodle the poor paper Dragon does not care to be made into a chicken coop and besides, when you capture him, can't you see that delays us? How do you 'spect us to find Marggy's Daddy when you act this way?" Raggedy Ann said.

"I shall take the paper Dragon home anyway!" Mr. Doodle howled as he pulled the paper Dragon.

"If we catch hold of the paper Dragon and pull back we will only pull the Dragon in two again," Raggedy Ann said to Marggy's Mama. "What had we better do?"

"I had better fight Mr. Doodle and see which one wins the paper Dragon," said Raggedy Andy.

"Why not let me fight with Mr. Doodle?" the Dragon said in a wheezy voice.

"That would be silly," Mr. Doodle replied. "I have already captured the Dragon, so he cannot fight with me."

"That is quite true," Raggedy Ann agreed. "I guess Raggedy Andy will have to fight with Mr. Doodle, but you must promise not to fight too hard."

So after Raggedy Andy and Mr. Doodle had both promised to fight real easy-like, they rolled up their sleeves. Mr. Doodle had the best of it for a long time because he could stick out his tongue at Raggedy Andy, but Raggedy Andy could not stick out his tongue at Mr. Doodle because Raggedy Andy's mouth was just painted on and he did not have a tongue. Of course, Raggedy Andy would not have stuck out his tongue at Mr. Doodle, even if he had a tongue, for that is a very rude thing to do, as everyone knows. But after awhile Raggedy Andy tweeked Mr. Doodle's nose and because Raggedy Andy's nose was painted upon his face, Mr. Doodle could not tweek Raggedy Andy's nose. Mr. Doodle sat down on a log and howled and then, of course, Raggedy Andy won the fight.

"Hurrah! Now we can mend the paper Dragon with the glue the little man gave us and go in search of Marggy's Daddy!" Raggedy Ann cried as she jumped up and down.

After walking a long time Marggy's Mama opened the basket of lunch. "Shall we give Mr. Doodle any?" Marggy's Mama asked. "He has treated us so mean he does not deserve any!"

Really, Mr. Doodle did not deserve any, but he looked so hungry, Raggedy Ann and Raggedy Andy, after whispering together, told Mr. Doodle to sit between them on the log and they gave him some of the doughnuts. After they had finished eating the doughnuts Raggedy Andy said, "Now we can travel in search of Marggy's Daddy and Mr. Doodle cannot follow us."

"Indeed, I can!" Mr. Doodle cried. "Whenever you start, I shall start with you."

Raggedy Ann and Raggedy Andy said to Marggy and her Mama, "Come! Let's hurry!" and they walked away leaving Mr. Doodle sitting on the log.

Mr. Doodle had a very queer look upon his face, because he did not know why he could not follow them.

"I took some of the glue and put it upon the log between Raggedy Ann and me," Raggedy Andy explained to Marggy and her Mama. "And when Mr. Doodle sat upon the glue, of course he stuck fast so now we can mend the paper Dragon and ride upon his back. Then Mr. Doodle will not be able to run and catch up with us and we will soon find Marggy's Daddy!"

It had only taken Raggedy Ann and Raggedy Andy two minutes to mend the Dragon's tail with the glue the little man has given them and it was such fine glue, it stuck very fast. It was lots of fun riding through the woods upon the paper Dragon's back because the Dragon wiggled along so smoothly. And our friends could not feel a bump even when the Dragon wiggled over large stones.

"I'm glad we have escaped from Mr. Doodle," the Dragon said as he carried his friends along upon his back. "For if we do not have Mr. Doodle bothering us all the time I am sure we will soon find Marggy's Daddy."

Raggedy Ann and Raggedy Andy and Marggy and her Mama felt so happy they laughed and sang songs as the Dragon carried them through the lovely woods.

CHAPTER NINE

AFTER awhile Raggedy Ann turned to say something to Raggedy Andy, and there coming behind them was Mr. Doodle. "Oh dear! Here comes Mr. Doodle!" Raggedy Ann said.

Raggedy Andy turned and looked. "My goodness!" he cried. "I forgot and left my magic wooden sword and now Mr. Doodle is riding upon the magic wooden sword and will soon catch up with us!"

The Dragon, on hearing this wiggled faster than ever, so fast that the trees and bushes seemed to whiz by, but the paper dragon could not go as fast as the magic wooden sword and pretty soon Mr. Doodle caught up with them.

"Stop, or I'll cut off the dragon's tail!" Mr. Doodle shouted to Raggedy Ann and Raggedy Andy.

"You cannot use the magic sword to cut off the dragon's tail while you are riding upon the wooden sword," Raggedy Andy laughed.

"Of course I can't when I am riding upon the wooden sword," Mr. Doodle shouted. "But unless you stop, I shall climb from the wooden sword to the dragon's back and then cut off his tail!"

There isn't anything to do except stop," Raggedy Ann

said. "We do not care to have Mr. Doodle cut off your tail again," she said to the dragon.

"How did you get free from where you were glued to the log?" Raggedy Andy asked Mr. Doodle.

"When I saw you leaving me alone on the log I wiggled and twisted as hard as I could, trying to get loose, but I could not get free. Then I grew angry and cried and the

tears ran down my nose onto the log and melted the glue
When I got loose, didn't I laugh!"

"Why did you laugh, silly?" Marggy's mama wished to
know, as she opened her basket and gave cookies to everyone.

"I laughed because I saw that Raggedy Andy had left his
magic wooden sword and I knew I would soon catch up with
you! That's why I laughed!"

"Sit down on the log beside Raggedy Andy and me and
have some lunch, Mr. Doodle. We do not believe in being
unkind to you even if you have been mean to us," Raggedy
Ann said.

Mr. Doodle looked carefully to see if Raggedy Andy had
put more glue upon the log. "If you try to fool me again I
shall give you a hard thump, Raggedy Andy," Mr. Doodle said.

"Give Mr. Doodle a handful of cookies," Raggedy Andy
said to Marggy's mama and when Marggy's mama had done
this Raggedy Andy said, "Now give Mr. Doodle a large piece
of chocolate cake because he must be hungry!" Marggy's
mama did as Raggedy Andy said, so when Mr. Doodle reached
for the large piece of chocolate cake, he had to drop Raggedy

Andy's magic wooden sword, because Mr. Doodle had both hands full of cake and cookies.

"Whee!" Raggedy Andy cried as he picked up the magic wooden sword. "Now I have the wooden sword and Mr. Doodle cannot follow us. As soon as we finish eating our lunch, we will start again!"

This made Mr. Doodle feel so badly to think how easily Raggedy Andy had fooled him, he cried, and Raggedy Ann had to wipe the tears to keep them from spoiling Mr. Doodle's cake and cookies. Then Raggedy Ann wiped the crumbs from everyone's mouths and said, "It is time we hurried along."

So Raggedy Andy helped Marggy and her mama and Raggedy Ann upon the back of the paper dragon and then climbed up himself, "All right, Mister Paper Dragon!" Raggedy Andy called. "You can wiggle along through the woods as fast as you wish." Then the paper dragon started moving; slow at first, then faster and faster until he was going just as fast as it is possible for paper dragons to wiggle.

After they had ridden upon the Dragon's back for almost an hour, they came to a little house, and out across the road at the side of the house was a gate.

The Dragon came to a stop with his nose touching the gate, just as a man came out of the little house and said, "This is a toll gate, so you will have to pay one penny for each passenger and two pennies for the Dragon, if you wish to travel down the road."

"Dear me!" Raggedy Ann said to the man. "We haven't any pennies!"

"Then you must turn around and go back," the man said.

"But if we do not go further down the road, we shall never find Marggy's Daddy," Raggedy Ann said.

"That would be too bad," the man replied as he wiped the tears from his eyes. "But I must have a penny from each passenger and two for the Dragon before I can let you pass."

"I know what to do!" the Dragon cried. "I'll wiggle back the road and get a good start, then I'll jump right over the gate."

JOHNNY GRUELLE

"Oh no!" Raggedy Ann said. "That would be cheating if you did that! And every one knows it isn't fair to cheat. We must find the pennies somewhere."

"Hasn't that man back there any pennies?" the toll gate keeper asked as he pointed back towards the Dragon's tail. And when they looked back there sitting upon the dragon's tail they saw Mr. Doodle.

When he found that he was discovered riding upon the Dragon's tail, Mr. Doodle came up to the Dragon's head and asked, "How much is it, Mr. Tollgate Keeper?"

"One penny for each passenger and two pennies for the Dragon," the Tollgate Keeper replied.

Mr. Doodle looked through all his pockets but could only find two pennies, a shoe button and a wire nail, "Dear me!" Mr. Doodle said. "I only have two pennies and that is only enough to take the Dragon through the tollgate."

"What shall we do?" Marggy's mama asked. "We can never find Marggy's daddy unless we go farther down the road!"

The tollgate keeper took off his hat and scratched his head. Finally he said, "I'll tell you how we can let you go through the tollgate. You know we charge only for people who ride, so if you hop down from the Dragon's back, I will charge two pennies for the Dragon and the rest of you can walk through the tollgate."

"We are very glad that you happened to think of that before we turned back," Raggedy Andy laughed as he jumped from the Dragon's back and helped Marggy and her mama and Raggedy Ann down.

Marggy's mama gave the toll gate keeper six cookies and a piece of chocolate cake and this pleased the Tollgate Keeper so much he asked every one, except the Dragon, who was too large, into his house and gave them each a glass of soda water, for you see, the Tollgate Keeper owned a little store too, so that anyone passing could have candy and peanuts and popcorn and lollypops and ice cream sodas.

Then Mr. Doodle, who was very fond of ice cream sodas asked the Tollgate Keeper if he would trade a lot of soda water for the shoe button and wire nail.

The Tollgate Keeper said that he had always longed for a shoe button and a wire nail, so he gave every one a soda and a bag of peanuts and took the shoe button and wire nail.

"I really believe Mr. Doodle has forgotten he wanted to take the Dragon home for a chicken coop," Raggedy Ann whispered to Raggedy Andy.

"I believe so, too!" Raggedy Andy whispered in return to Raggedy Ann. "For if he had not paid the Tollgate Keeper the two pennies to get the Dragon through the tollgate, he could have taken the Dragon away from us again."

But Raggedy Andy did not remind Mr. Doodle of this. Mr. Doodle laughed and talked with everyone and said he was sorry he did not have another shoe button and a wire nail he could trade for more sodas and peanuts.

"Well," Mr. Doodle said, when he had finished drinking the last of his soda. "I guess we had better be going on, or it will be late before we find Marggy's Daddy!"

After shaking hands with the kind Tollgate Keeper the Dragon carried them through the woods until they came to a great marble castle.

CHAPTER TEN

IN FRONT of the great marble castle stood a Knight all dressed in shiny armor and he had a great big shiny sword. When the Dragon stopped in front of the Knight, the Knight whirled his sword close to the Dragon's nose.

"Please be careful, Mr. Knight," Raggedy Ann said. "You might cut off the Dragon's nose."

"Ha!" the Knight laughed as he whirled his sword again. "Little would I care if I did! We have a prisoner shut up in the castle and I must guard the door so that no one can get in and rescue him."

"I'll bet a nickel the prisoner is Marggy's Daddy," Mr. Doodle said.

"It is!" the Knight cried. "And if you know what is good for you, you will turn around and run as fast as you can!"

"Please do be careful," Raggedy Ann again said. "You almost whacked the paper Dragon that time! It wouldn't be nice for you to cut off his nose even if it is only paper!"

"Then if you will hop down from the Dragon's back, I will cut off your nose," the Knight said to Raggedy Ann.

"Indeed you won't," Raggedy Ann laughed. "For my nose is merely painted upon my face and it can't be cut off."

"Then I will cut off that man's nose," the Knight said as he pointed his sword at Mr. Doodle.

"But I do not care to have my nose cut off!"

"Then I shall cut off your nose anyhow!" The Knight shouted. "So if you do not wish your nose cut off you had better run as fast as you know how!"

"I will not run a step!" Mr. Doodle cried. "And if you try to cut off my nose, I shall try to cut off your nose too, only you will have to lend me your sword."

"Ha, ha, ha!" the Knight laughed. "I would be foolish to do that! You have a sword," pointing to Raggedy Andy's wooden sword. "Take that and we will have a grand fight to see which one cuts off the other's nose."

Raggedy Andy loaned Mr. Doodle his magic wooden sword and Mr. Doodle walked towards the Knight.

"Wait a minute," the Knight said. "Someone will have to fasten my helmet down so Mr. Doodle cannot cut off my nose!"

"That is only fair," Mr. Doodle replied. "For I know you do not wish your nose cut off any more than I wish mine cut off, so I will fasten your helmet."

"There!" Mr. Doodle said when he finished fastening the Knight's helmet. "Now I cannot even see your eyes."

"But I cannot see out of the helmet either!" the Knight howled. "And how can I fight you when I can't see?"

"Well!" Mr. Doodle replied. "You said you wanted the helmet fastened down tight so now you will have to make the best of it!" And as Mr. Doodle winked at Raggedy Andy, he hit the Knight's helmet so hard with the wooden sword it sounded like someone had kicked a tin dish pan.

"Oh! My nose! Oh, my nose!" the Knight howled and every time he howled, Mr. Doodle hit the Knight's helmet harder than ever with the wooden sword until the Knight threw down his shiny sword and cried, "Let's quit fighting! I have changed my mind, I shall not cut off your nose!"

"Thank you!" Mr. Doodle said as he winked at Raggedy Ann and unfastened the Knight's helmet.

"My goodness! I did not know anyone could fight so good with just a wooden sword!" the Knight said. "You won the fight very quickly!"

"Maybe if you had not fastened your helmet down over your eyes, you could have won the fight," Mr. Doodle said. "Shall we try it again without the helmet?"

"No, thank you," the Knight replied. "I feel certain that if I do not have the helmet fastened down tight over my face you will be sure to cut off my nose. You see, I try to frighten people away from the castle by pretending that I am a great fighter, but really, I am always very timid, for I have a real tender heart."

"And you did not intend cutting off Mr. Doodle's nose?" Raggedy Ann asked.

"Dear me, no!" the Knight laughed. "You see, I shut my eyes anyway when I fight, so I could not have cut off Mr. Doodle's nose for I could not have seen it!"

"I am glad you are so kind hearted," Raggedy Ann said. "Really, that is the best way to be anyhow."

"That is just what my mama has always told me," the Knight said. "And now that Mr. Doodle has won the fight there is nothing to keep you from going into the castle unless it is the two-headed dog just inside the door. He may jump out and chase you away when you open the door."

"We will go and knock upon the door," Mr. Doodle said. "Then if the two-headed dog barks, we will know enough not to open the door."

"Oh, he barks something terrible," the Knight said. "It makes cold chills run up my neck when I hear him bark."

"You don't 'spect the two-headed dog has eaten up my daddy, do you?" Marggy asked.

"Oh, my no!" the Knight replied. "I saw your daddy looking out of a window awhile ago! No! The two-headed dog hasn't eaten him up."

Mr. Doodle walked up to the door and the Dragon wiggled along with the others.

"Why! There is the little ball of red darning cotton!" Raggedy Ann cried as she pointed to the door step. "Please hand it to me, Mr. Doodle; it got away ahead of us when you delayed us so many times!"

"I am very sorry!" Mr. Doodle said as he handed the ball of red darning cotton to Raggedy Ann.

"Knock on the door, it wouldn't be polite to walk in without knocking," Raggedy Andy suggested. "What we want to do is to get in the castle and rescue Marggy's Daddy who has been inside as a prisoner for so long, but if the dog barks then we are as bad off as we are now."

"I know what to do," Mr. Doodle suggested. "Let's hammer upon the castle door with the wooden sword and the two-headed dog will stay at the door in hopes that we will open it and let him out, but we will fool him! While someone hammers on the door and keeps the two-headed dog there I will run around in back and climb up the water pipe to one of the windows, then I'll tip-toe down and throw a blanket, or something, over the dog's two heads and unlock the door for you to come in!"

"That is a good idea," Raggedy Ann said. "Let's go and hammer on the door with the wooden sword."

The Dragon carried them all up to the door of the castle upon his back and Raggedy Andy hammered upon the castle door with his magic wooden sword. WHACK! WHACK! WHACK!

Then they heard the loudest barks they had ever heard from a dog.

"My goodness!" Raggedy Ann cried. "He must be very, very large to bark so loud! I am afraid if you climb up the pipes and tip-toe down to throw something over the dog's two heads, you will not find a blanket large enough!"

"I have a better idea," the Dragon said. "Mr. Doodle might fall and hurt himself. I will open my mouth as wide as I can, then when you open the door, the great two headed dog will jump right out into my mouth, then I'll close my mouth and we will have him a prisoner!"

"Hm!" mused Raggedy Andy. "Suppose the two-headed

dog starts scratching and biting after he jumps into your mouth?"

"I won't mind that!" the Dragon replied. "You can get inside the door long before he tears the paper off my sides and gets out, and I will be glad to do this for Marggy's sake."

So the Dragon opened his mouth so wide it covered the whole door and Raggedy Andy poked the magic wooden sword between the Dragon's paper teeth and pushed the castle door open. There came five very, very, loud barks as the two-headed dog jumped out of the door into the Dragon's mouth. Then the Dragon's mouth closed shut with a snap and the two-headed dog was a prisoner.

MY! How the two-headed dog scratched around inside the Dragon. He made a lot of noise, because the Dragon was made of slats and covered with heavy paper.

"Now we must jump off the Dragon's back and hunt through the castle until we find Marggy's Daddy. And we must hurry before the great two-headed dog chews the paper out of the Dragon's side and chases us!" Raggedy Ann cried.

"After we find Marggy's Daddy, then the Dragon can open his mouth and let the two-headed dog out, for after we find Marggy's Daddy, then, of course, there will be no reason for the dog guarding the door, and he will probably run around the castle and hunt for a bone to eat!" Mr. Doodle said.

"Maybe it would be a good plan giving the dog a bone before we go into the castle," Raggedy Ann suggested. "For if the dog has something to eat, then he won't tear the paper off of the Dragon's wooden slats." Everyone thought this was a good idea. Raggedy Ann usually thought of the best way of doing everything. But, of course, when they looked through all their pockets, not even Mr. Doodle had a bone.

"We will have to give the two-headed dog a large piece of chocolate cake," Marggy's Mama said. "All I have in my basket is cake and cookies and I do not believe that will be enough for such a large two-headed dog."

"Then we must give him two pieces of chocolate cake," said Raggedy Ann. "One for each head."

So Marggy's Mama cut off two large pieces of chocolate cake and told the Dragon to open his mouth. "Just as soon as the great two-headed dog sees that he can get out, then he will quit his loud barking and I will throw him the cake," she said.

So the Dragon opened his mouth and Marggy's Mama tossed the two pieces of cake where the two-headed dog could see them.

"Look out!" the Dragon cried, "He's coming out!" and out from the Dragon's mouth came the two-headed dog.

When Raggedy Ann saw the two-headed dog, she jumped from the Dragon's back and caught the dog in her arms, for the two-headed dog which guarded the castle door with such a loud bark was only six inches high, and the cutest little creature the Raggedys had ever seen.

Raggedy Ann held the two-headed dog in her arms while Raggedy Andy and Marggy and her Mama and Mr. Doodle fed him small pieces of cookies and chocolate cake. My! How Raggedy Ann laughed!

After the two-headed dog had eaten all the cake he wanted, Raggedy Ann wiped the crumbs from his two mouths with her apron and said, "Now that we have discovered that the two-headed dog is only a little teeny, weeny dog we can take him with us through the castle and hunt for Marggy's Daddy!"

"I will be glad to go with you," the two-headed dog said out of both of his mouths at the same time. "For I know just where Marggy's Daddy is!"

"It is funny that the people who own this castle had such a tiny, little two-headed dog to guard the door," Raggedy Andy said.

"But, you see," the little two-headed dog explained. "I have just about the largest bark in the world, and when I stand at the door and bark, whoever is outside thinks, 'Goodness gracious! That must be a very large dog!' And of course that frightens them away!"

"Yes," agreed Raggedy Ann. "We thought you must be almost as large as a horse when we heard you bark. Are you a magic dog?"

"Oh, yes," the little two-headed dog replied. "Everything in the castle is magic. That is why Marggy's Daddy stays at the castle instead of going home."

"I do not understand!" Marggy's Mama said. "Why does he have to stay at the magic castle, little two-headed dog?"

"Because," the little dog replied. "When Marggy's Daddy is in the castle, he can remember you and Marggy and everyone he knew before, but just as soon as he starts to go out of the castle door, he loses his memory and while he is outside the castle he forgets about everyone he knew. So you see he stays in the castle so that he can always remember you."

"Then," Raggedy Ann wondered. "Perhaps we had better not go inside the magic castle, or we may lose our memory."

"No," the little dog said. "The magic only works on people who enter the castle on Monday."

"If that is the case, let us all go inside, for today is Wednesday," Mr. Doodle cried. "And when we are once inside, perhaps we can find Marggy's Daddy's memory and give it back to him after we get him outside of the magic castle."

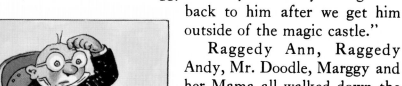

Raggedy Ann, Raggedy Andy, Mr. Doodle, Marggy and her Mama all walked down the long hall and through an open door, and there, sitting in a comfortable chair was Marggy's Daddy. Marggy and her Mama ran to him and threw their arms about him, but he looked so surprised, everyone knew that Marggy's Daddy did not know Marggy and her Mama.

"Don't you recognize Marggy and her Mama?" Raggedy Ann asked.

"No! I cannot remember ever seeing them before!" Marggy's Daddy replied.

CHAPTER ELEVEN

"I'LL just bet a nickel that he has lost his memory around the castle somewhere," Raggedy Andy said.

"But I had my memory when I came in a few minutes ago!" Marggy's Daddy said.

"Well! You haven't it now!" Raggedy Ann replied. "So tell us just where you have been about the castle and we will try and find your memory for you."

So Marggy's Daddy led the way to the Wonder Room, but no one could find his memory. Then they searched through the dining room, but it was not there!

"I had it when I came in the back door," Marggy's Daddy said.

Raggedy Ann ran to the easy chair where they had first seen Marggy's Daddy and there, sticking between the pages of a book to mark the place where he had been reading, was Marggy's Daddy's memory. Then everyone was very happy and Marggy's Daddy took them all on his lap and hugged them, even Mr. Doodle.

"Tell us how you happened to be a prisoner in the magic castle, Daddy," Marggy said as she gave him a hug.

"One day," Marggy's Daddy began, "I kissed Marggy and her Mama good-bye and started down to the store and when I came to a great tree which had fallen across the road, I heard someone talking inside."

"Who was it, Daddy?" Marggy wished to know.

"It was a little gnome, sitting there smoking his pipe and talking to himself," Marggy's Daddy went on. "And I heard him talking about a wonderful Magic Castle, with a great room in it called the Wonder Room. And I heard him tell just how to find the Magic Castle. So instead of going to the grocery I walked through the woods until I came to this castle. The two-headed dog barked so loud at the front door, I went around to the back door and as it was open, I walked right inside. But whenever I went outside of the castle, I lost my memory. So I couldn't think to return to Marggy and her Mama. But when I came back into the Magic Castle, then I could remember them. So, rather than leave the castle and forget them, I had to stay here all the time, so that I could think of them."

"Now that we have found you, Daddy," Marggy's Mama said, "Let's return home!"

"That is just what I was thinking of," Marggy's Daddy replied. "And just as soon as I pack a few magic things in a suit case, we will start. I have found so many wonderful magic things in the Wonder Room, I hardly know which to take home."

Of course, everyone wished to know what the wonderful things were, so Marggy's Daddy told them. "There is a magic clock," he said, "which strikes every five minutes. And as soon as it quits striking, it either tells a fairy story, or it sings a beautiful song. Then this book which I was reading when you came in is a wonderful book, too, for, while you read the story, you can see moving pictures of everything you read about. Then when you grow tired of reading yourself, it will read itself, right out loud!"

"That will be a nice book for Marggy to have," Marggy's Mama said.

"Yes, we must take it for Marggy," Marggy's Daddy agreed.

"Then, the magic soda water fountain in the Wonder

Room. We need it in our front room so that we can give everyone who comes in a nice ice cream soda. Then, there is a whole case of wonderful wishing rings. We each need one. And there is a wonderful invisible cloak, which makes anyone invisible. Then there are magical roller skates, which when fastened to your shoes, will carry you around as fast, or as slow as you wish to go."

Then Marggy's Daddy got a very large suitcase, for it had to be very large to get all the magical things inside. Everyone helped Marggy's Daddy pack the magical things in the suitcase.

"Now, I guess we are all ready to start," Marggy's Daddy laughed as he took the suitcase upon his shoulder.

"What have you in the suitcase?" the Dragon asked as he saw Marggy's Daddy with the suitcase on his shoulder.

"Some wonderful things I picked up inside," Marggy's Daddy replied. Then a queer look came over his face and he put the suitcase upon the ground and opened it.

"I thought so!" he cried. "I felt it suddenly grow light, and it had been so heavy before; all the wonderful things have disappeared!"

"The magic soda water fountain, too?" Marggy asked.

"Yes! It has disappeared, too! Now we can't take them home and enjoy them!"

"Well!" Raggedy Andy mused. "It seems to me that the wonderful Magic Castle has been made so that whoever enters the Magic Castle can enjoy the wonderful magical things in the Wonder Room, but if everyone who goes into the Magic Castle carries away some of the wonderful things, in a very short time, there would be nothing left. And so, the magical things always come back to the Wonder Room."

"That is so!" agreed Marggy's Daddy. "And it was not right for us to take them."

"Indeed, it wasn't," Raggedy Andy said. "You must keep the wonderful magic castle for your home."

"Whee! Whee!" Marggy's Daddy cried, "Raggedy Andy

has thought of the nicest way! We will all live in the magic Castle where we can all enjoy the magic things in the Wonder Room; the magic soda water fountain, the wishing rings, the talking books, the magic clock and all the other wonderful things, and Raggedy Ann and Raggedy Andy and Mr. Doodle and the Dragon can live here with us!"

They all caught hold of hands and danced around in a circle. All except Mr. Doodle, and as everyone looked at Mr. Doodle, they saw great big salty tears running down his nose and falling to the ground. "Why, Mr. Doodle!" Raggedy Ann cried, "Whatever is the trouble?"

It was a long time before Mr. Doodle could reply and it would have been much longer than that if Marggy's Mama hadn't given him a piece of chocolate cake out of her basket. After Mr. Doodle had eaten the chocolate cake, Raggedy Ann said, "Tell us why you weep, Mr. Doodle."

"Because," Mr. Doodle replied. "Because, you will remember, I wanted to take the paper Dragon home and use him for a chicken coop. He is hollow all the way to the tip of his tail, and he would make a lovely chicken coop. But now, I know the paper Dragon is such a kind creature, I do not wish to take him away from you and take him home, besides, if I did that, there would be no one to guard the outside doors of the Magic Castle."

"But," Marggy's Mama said, "You are going to stay

right here in the wonderful Magic Castle with us, and if you do that, there is no need of you having a chicken coop. For, every time you wish fried chicken, all you will have to do will be to wish for it and you will have it. Isn't that so, Daddy?"

"Indeed, it is true," Marggy's Daddy replied. "So dry your tears, Mr. Doodle and live with us in the Magic Castle and we will have a lot of fun."

"Then I must run home and get Mrs. Doodle," Mr. Doodle said as he wiped the last tear from his eye.

"Do not pack anything in your suitcases," Marggy's Daddy advised. "For if you, or Mrs. Doodle, want new clothes any time, all you have to do is wish for them."

"I shall not bring a thing except Mrs. Doodle," Mr. Doodle laughed. "Now just see how fast I can run home and return with Mrs. Doodle."

"I'll bet a nickel it won't take him very long," Raggedy

Andy laughed, as they watched Mr. Doodle run away through the woods toward his home.

In a very short time Mr. Doodle came running back with Mrs. Doodle, for he had hardly got started running through the woods when he met Mrs. Doodle coming after him.

"I just thought Mr. Doodle never would come home," Mrs. Doodle laughed when she was introduced to everyone. "Is it true that you wish Mr. Doodle and me to live in this beautiful castle with you, even after Mr. Doodle and I treated you so mean?"

"Yes, indeed, Mrs. Doodle!" Marggy's Mama said. "You see, Mr. Doodle has changed quite a lot since you saw him last, and if it had not been for his kindness to us, we would never have found our nice Daddy."

"Then I am so happy!" Mrs. Doodle said as she wept on Raggedy Ann's shoulder. "Papa Doodle has always been a very lazy Papa and that was one reason why he always wanted to capture Marggy. He really wanted her to do the work!"

"And I know just how naughty I was, Mama Doodle," Mr. Doodle said. "And I have promised myself that I shall chop every piece of wood we need in the nice, wonderful Magical Castle to cook with."

"Aha!" Marggy's Daddy laughed as he gave Mr. Doodle a friendly thump upon the back. "We will need no wood around here to cook with, my friend, for if we wish fried chicken or doughnuts or anything, we do not have to build a fire and cook. No, sir!"

So Marggy's Daddy led the way into the dining room of the castle and everyone wished for just whatever they liked best for supper. And you may be certain that everyone got exactly what they wished for, too, because that was the way things worked in the wonderful castle. After supper, everyone went into the Wonder Room and listened to the Magic Book as it read fairy tales out loud, and while they listened to the fairy tales they all had a great many ice cream sodas.

"It is really time we were all getting to bed," Marggy's Daddy said. "The earlier we go to bed, the earlier we can get up in the morning, and think how much fun we shall have then."

Marggy's Daddy knew every room in the great castle, so he showed everyone just where to sleep, then when he had wound the clock and covered up the canary bird and saw the little two-headed dog had gone to his box, Marggy's Daddy went to bed, too.

"Wasn't it just like a Fairy Tale?" Raggedy Ann asked Raggedy Andy as they put on their nighties and hopped into bed.

"Indeed, it was, Raggedy Ann," Raggedy Andy laughed. "And I 'spect, just like all nice Fairy Tales, everyone will live happily together here in the wonderful Magic Castle forever."

And the two Raggedys, their shiny shoe button eyes looking happily at the ceiling, felt in their little cotton stuffed bodies that indeed, this would prove true, for unhappiness can never creep in when hearts are filled with the sunshine of unselfish love.

Look for these other Raggedy Ann Books

MY FIRST RAGGEDY ANN